WHISTLE STOP IN SPACE

THE FURTHER ADVENTURES OF MANNING DRACO, VOLUME 2

Wendell F. Crossen

WHISTLE STOP IN SPACE

THE FURTHER ADVENTURES OF MANNING DRACO, VOLUME 2

KENDELL FOSTER CROSSEN

ILLUSTRATIONS BY
VIRGIL FINLAY &
ALEX SCHOMBURG

FOREWORD BY
KENDRA CROSSEN BURROUGHS

ALTUS PRESS • 2013

Published by Altus Press

EDITED AND DESIGNED BY
Matthew Moring
Visit altuspress.com for more books like this.

PUBLISHING HISTORY
The featured stories were originally published as follows. They have been edited by Kendra Crossen Burroughs for this edition.
"Whistle Stop in Space," *Thrilling Wonder Stories,* vol. 42, no. 3 (August 1953). Illustrated by Virgil Finlay.
"Mission to Mizar," *Thrilling Wonder Stories,* vol. 43, no. 1 (November 1953). Illustrated by Alex Schomburg.
"The Agile Algolian," *Thrilling Wonder Stories,* vol. 43, no. 2 (Winter 1954). Illustrated by Virgil Finlay.

Printed in the United States of America.

ISBN: 978-1-61827-103-7

For

EMILY

Brave New Terran

CONTENTS

FOREWORD

MEET MANNING DRACO, stalwart son of planet Terra, the Galaxy's greatest gumshoe. If you read *Once Upon a Star*, volume one of the Manning Draco adventures, you know that Manning was chief investigator for the Greater Solarian Insurance Company, Monopolated, during which time he and his boss, J. Barnaby Cruikshank, fought almost continually. By book's end, Manning, a world-class skirt-chaser, had tied the knot with the boss's daughter and launched his own business—the Draco Vacation Service—to support his wife and bonny little son. Meanwhile, his father-in-law was invited to become Secretary of Planets in the Federation Cabinet.

Now Manning is back in three new stories, never before published in book form.

It is the multicultural cosmos of the 3470s, when the beings of numerous planetary systems mingle together throughout the Galactic Federation. The quaint customs and ancient laws of some 107 planets are bound to clash at times. Despite much ceremonial shaking of hands, tentacles, and tails, the Achernarians hate the Regulusians, the Capellans hate the Polluxians, the Procyonese hate the Arcturusians, the Vegans hate the Achernarians—and there are groups from Terra who hate everyone except themselves. All of this makes for some little clambake, as Manning Draco observed. Manning wishes he had nothing more to worry about than the vacation problems of a honeymooning threesome from Sirius. But his father-in-law has other plans for him.

In the opening story, "Whistle Stop in Space," a Galactic election is coming up, and it is essential that the Republocrats stay in power. To ensure the election is not sabotaged by an Acruxian agent who has infiltrated Regulus, J. Barnaby sends Manning to pose as an election observer and stop the Acruxian in whatever he's doing. But Manning's worst challenge might be to resist the advances of a certain golden-eyed humanoid from Aldebaran IV, whose charms conceal a rather shocking surprise.

In "Mission to Mizar," an Acruxian agent provocateur is once more fomenting rebellion, this time on a planet that is just about to join the Federation. If Mizar should withdraw its membership, it could mean war—and one wouldn't want to be at war with the Mizarians, the only race capable of anticipating an opponent's next move (a talent known as cryptesthesia). As the only Terran who has ever developed a secondary mind shield, Manning Draco is the man to stand up against the telepathic Acruxian. So off he goes in his space cruiser to straighten out the situation. Things get a tad complicated when a comely, blue-haired female with orange eyes turns out to be a stowaway on board.

The final story, "The Agile Algolian," takes us back in time to 3470, when our hero was an insurance detective and a single man, to at last explain how Manning became the only Terran ever to develop a secondary mind shield against telepathic probes. The story includes a wacky spoof of Mickey Spillane's Mike Hammer, in the person of "Mickey Hatchet."

An alert to pun lovers: Ken Crossen planted some groaners here based on foreign words: for example, Par Egzanpl (from French *par example*) and Insta Tuquo (after Latin *in statu quo*, "in the same state"). A few are derived from Yiddish. The son of Southern Baptists from rural Ohio, Crossen became an ardent Hebrophile; the pseudonym "M.E. Chaber," under which he penned the Milo March detective series of the 1950s–1970s, derives from *mechaber,* the Hebrew word for "author," and Ken sometimes signed his letters "Shmendrick." It must have delighted him to give characters in the Manning Draco series such names as "Dr. Boichik" (from the sarcastic or affectionate Yiddish diminutive of "boy") and Pisha Paisha, after a Yiddish card game. A sprinkling of parodies of the Advertising Age ("When you see something you want and can't have, does your tongue hang out? If so, buy Meehel's Patented Tongue-Shrinker") still ring true in our product-obsessed society.

Once again, on behalf of the Crossen descendants, I thank Matt Moring of Altus Press for helping to bring our father's work to a new audience.

Kendra Crossen Burroughs

PROLOG

L IKE LEAVES on trees the race of man is found. Galaxy I, the
erstwhile Milky Way, contains almost one million planets
known to be inhabited by intelligent beings. Among the most
interesting, for our purposes, is Earth, the third planet in the
system of Sol, which became known as Terra at the beginning
of the twenty-second century.

The Terrans advanced rapidly, and in an incredible span of
some three thousand years, the planet raced through primitive
dictatorships, primitive and advanced monarchies, republics,
and democracies, totalitarian rules of the Left, Right, and
Middle, and finally achieved an equalitarian one-world government in 2164 following a 200-year war that almost destroyed
the planet.

Space flights were being made between several star systems in
the galaxy by 2200. The first contacts between planets were tenta-
tive and marked by considerable hesitation on the part of everyone.
Behind this diffidence, however, each planet was scheming to
conquer the others. As a natural result, interplanetary war broke
out in the spring of 2306 between Terra, Mars, Vega I, Rigel IV,
and Dubhe III. As the galactic battle entered its second century,
fifteen other planets, having attained space flight, declared war on
one side or the other. For 600 years the battle raged across the
galaxy, and the damage and loss of life stagger the imagination.
Finally, in the year 3014, the war was suddenly ended following a
secret agreement between Terra, Mars, Vega, Sirius, and Procyon.

Shortly after peace was restored, Terra, once more backed by Mars, Vega, Sirius, and Procyon, formed the Galactic Federation, which they have dominated since that time.

In the early years the Federation was what might be described as a loose democracy, and during that time it grew to include almost a hundred planets. Then the Terran bloc pulled the coup of 3453, and the first monopolist government came into power. A young man named J. Barnaby Cruikshank played an important role in the shift of political power and received the first monopoly charter to be granted by the new government.

The year that J. Barnaby Cruikshank achieved the status of a federation monopolist, Manning Draco had just entered Solar University on Rigel Kentaurus. Those two shady characters, the Terran Sam Warren and the Rigelian Dzanku Dzanku, had just begun their capers in crime. Manning first encountered them in *Once Upon a Star*, volume 1 of the Draco adventures, and they rear their crooked heads once again in volume 2.

By the age of forty, J. Barnaby Cruikshank was president and chief stockholder of the Greater Solarian Insurance Company, Monopolated, a company based in Nyork that spanned two galaxies. When he inherited the original small firm from his grandfather, it insured only humans and confined its operations to Earth. Under the direction of J. Barnaby, policies had been issued to cover all forms of life on every planet.

Since J. Barnaby was also influential in Federation politics, the Earth corporation had soon achieved an intergalactic monopoly charter, and Manning Draco, as his chief investigator, enjoyed limited police powers throughout the galaxies. After Manning married the boss's daughter, Vega Cruikshank, and left the insurance company to form his own interplanetary travel agency, it was only natural that his father–in–law felt free to draft him to represent the Federation whenever emergencies arose in the conduct of governmental affairs.

As Manning was soon to learn, when duty calls, chaos is just around the corner....

ACT ONE / SUMMER 3473

WHISTLE STOP
IN SPACE

CHAPTER ONE

THE DRACO VACATION SERVICE occupied one floor in Interplanetary Towers in Nyork. The seventy-second floor, to be exact. It had been decorated by one of the best robot-decorators in the Federation and looked it. On one wall of the large reception room there was a three-dimensional mural of Caph II. The blue sand and towering purple trees seemed so real that many of the more bucolic visitors bumped into the wall before they realized it was a painting. In front of the mural there was a fountain spouting the pink water of Caph that tasted like champagne.

On another wall was a montage of photographs of Caph, and blazoned across it:

YOU CAN CHEAT TIME BY VACATIONING ON SUNNY CAPH, THE PLAYLAND OF THE UNIVERSE. A TWO-WEEK VACATION IS TEN MONTHS ON CAPH. THE ONLY PLACE IN THE GALAXY WHERE LIFE PAYS YOU TWENTY-TO-ONE. YOU OWE CAPH TO YOURSELF.

Business was rushing, as it had been every day since the Draco Vacation Service had opened. Despite the fact that there weren't enough tour-managers to take care of the crowd, and that there was a Fomalhautan millionaire who thought it was demeaning to discuss his vacation with anyone except the president, it was

only two o'clock when Manning Draco left his private office. He stopped for a moment beside the receptionist, an attractive Martian female. There were at least a dozen persons crowded around her as she answered their questions. Manning stood by her desk, apparently paying no attention to her.

Dhena, he thought, *I have to leave. It's possible that I may be gone several days. Paul Sterling will be in charge.* This was the chief reason he had hired a Martian receptionist. Telepathic communication was a great advantage when you didn't want to be overheard.

Yes, Mr. Draco. Her answering thought was clear and strong as she continued to deal with the questions of would-be vacationists. *Where will you be if we need you?*

With my back against a wall, if I know anything about it, he thought sourly. He walked across the office and took the level converter. Downstairs, he climbed into an aircab and gave the driver the address of his home.

Manning Draco no longer lived in the tiny bachelor apartment he had once called home. Draco Vacation Service, started shortly after he had married Vega Cruikshank, had prospered right from the beginning and he had rented a modest pent-estate in the Upper East Side. The house, built on top of one

of the giant apartment buildings, was modern in every respect and was surrounded by two acres of landscaped grounds.

Vega came running out to meet him as the cab deposited him on the landing strip in front of the house.

"Darling," she exclaimed, giving him a kiss, "you remembered and came home early."

"Remembered?" Manning asked, looking blank.

"Barnaby is five months old today," she said proudly. "You mean that isn't why you came home early?" Barnaby was, of course, Manning's and Vega's son who had been born on Caph II. He had been named after J. Barnaby Cruikshank, his grandfather, the president of the Greater Solarian Insurance Company, Monopolated, for whom Manning—in his own words—had given the best years of his life. At the age of five months, young Barnaby produced a number of gurgling sounds which Manning swore were pure Capellanese.

"I remembered his birthday," Manning said, momentarily forgetting his gloom. "I ordered him a set of atomic trains. Haven't they been delivered yet?"

"Oh, Manning," Vega said, laughing, as they went into the house. "Atomic trains. He won't be able to play with those for another six years."

"Not Barnaby," Manning declared. "He's a smart kid. He'll have them in operation before you know it."

Vega laughed again.

"But that's not the reason I'm home early," Manning said darkly.

"Sit down and relax and then you'll tell me all about it," Vega said soothingly. "Have you heard the wonderful news about Father? After all these years of making big contributions to the Republocrats, he's finally been given the sort of reward he's wanted. He's been made Secretary of Planets."

"That," Manning said grimly, "is why I'm home early."

VEGA RECOGNIZED the tone, although she couldn't imagine

what was causing it. She slipped her hand in his and waited.

"I don't know what he's up to," Manning said, "but you can be sure that it's something I won't like. He called and told me the news this afternoon. I knew it was something he'd always wanted and so I poured on a little flattery. I told him that I thought it was pretty generous of him to take time from his business to devote his talents to government. I even mentioned that the Federation should have more public-spirited citizens like him."

"That must have pleased him."

"Ha!" said Manning without humor. "He said he was glad that I felt that way because he had a job for me to do and he would expect me in his office on Rigel Kentaurus at three-thirty this afternoon."

"Oh," said Vega. Now she understood. "But you can't possibly leave the business now, darling! This is the middle of the vacation season."

"I explained those things to him," Manning said bitterly. "His only answer was to tell me that as Secretary of Planets he has the right to draft any citizen for special emergency jobs. He said that if I wasn't in his office by three-thirty, he'd send the police after me. He would, too."

"What are you going to do?"

"Go to Rigil Kentaurus. On the way, I'm going to try to figure out some way of legally removing a father-in-law. Come on, help me pack. I'd better take a few things. When your father has something he wants me to do, I'm liable to need anything from an extra pair of socks to a few spare lives."

"All right, darling," Vega said. She followed him into their bedroom. "But if Daddy sends you chasing off to some strange planet, remember one thing, Manning Draco. No girls—not even platonic ones. No reverting to type."

"You wrong me, dear," Manning said in wounded tones. "I never chased after women in my life. They chased me. Take, for example, that lovely girl, the former Vega—"

"All right," Vega interrupted, "only be sure that you run faster than you did when I chased you."

"I can't help it if I'm irresistible to women," Manning purred as he ducked the shoe she aimed at him.

A few minutes later, a vacuum-packed traveling case under his arm, Manning Draco bestowed a brief kiss on his sleeping son, a longer one on his wife, and took an aircab to the Nyork spaceport. He had phoned them from the office so that his space cruiser, the *Alpha Actuary,* was already on the launching rack. He climbed in, cleared with the control tower, and blasted off.

When he reached the edge of atmosphere, he threw the ship into magnidrive for the ten-minute run to Rigil Kentaurus.

At exactly three-thirty Manning Draco was in the Planet Department building, being shown into the office of the Secretary.

At forty-one, J. Barnaby Cruikshank was one of the most successful men in' the Galaxy. He had originally inherited the Greater Solarian Insurance Company from his grandfather, but it had been a small company barely making a profit. J. Barnaby had built it up until its assets were somewhere around one and a half trillion credits. He had been very active in galactic politics, and much of his success was due to that, but this was the first time he'd been given active participation in the government.

J. Barnaby had always operated on the theory that chaos was just around the corner. Those who worked for Greater Solarian— as Manning had until only a few months before—were accustomed to J. Barnaby's looking as though the corner had finally been rounded. So the rumpled appearance of the new Secretary of Planets had no effect on Manning.

AS HE ENTERED the office, he caught a glimpse of another man leaving by a side door. He was a Vegan, his skin the clear green of old jade. The weave of his light plastic suit indicated that he was a high-caste Vegan.

"Who was that?" Manning asked.

"Jimwe Gnade. Harris is being made an ambassador and the

Vegan is going to be the new candidate for vice president."

"Great Fomalhaut," exclaimed Manning. "Now we're even going to have political candidates who contain chlorophyll."

"Very funny," grunted J. Barnaby. "How're Vega and little Barnaby?"

"How do you expect them to be, losing husband and father just so you can make a big man out of yourself?"

"You've decided to do the job?" J. Barnaby asked, ignoring the remark.

"Do I have a choice?"

"Not much," J. Barnaby said with a familiar grin. "The penalty for refusing a government draft is five years."

"Little Barnaby," said Manning, "will have enough trouble living down the fact that he has you for a grandfather, so he'll need my fatherly guidance. I'll do it."

"My dear Manning," J. Barnaby said expansively, "I knew I could count on you. I've always known that there was a heart of gold beneath that—er—plain exterior. I knew I could depend on you to put aside personal considerations—"

"Don't try to make such a big thing out of it," Manning interrupted. "I said I'd do it. Now what is it you want?"

"Do you know Regulus II?"

"I know of it, but I've never been there."

"You will be, my boy, before the day is over. You, of course, know, that for years the Federation has been bothered by Acrux and its satellite systems. They have constantly tried to stir up trouble among the member planets of the Federation, as well as trying to provoke incidents which might give them an excuse to invade us. Well, an Acruxian agent is now on Regulus II."

"Why tell *me* about it?" Manning asked. "Sounds like a job for the Federation police."

"As a matter of fact," Barnaby said in what he imagined was a confidential tone, "this is a pretty delicate situation and I doubt if the average policeman could handle it. Then, there are reasons why there might be complaints if the matter is handled by a regular government representative."

"What reasons?" Manning asked bluntly. His eyes narrowed with suspicion. "And while you're at it, you might also explain what your special angle is."

"My dear Manning, my only motivation is that of the responsibility of my great office—"

"Meteor dust," snapped Manning. "Tell me the whole thing or I'll let you go ahead and put me in jail."

When he saw that Manning wouldn't give in, the pained expression faded from J. Barnaby's face. "As a matter of fact," he said, "there is a slight political aspect to the problem. As you know, there is a galactic election coming up. I should like to continue to serve as Secretary of Planets, but this will be possible only if the Republocrats are re-elected. It looks as if it might be a close race."

"And what does that have to do with Regulus and the Acruxian agent you say is there?"

"Everything," J. Barnaby said simply. "Regulus was admitted to the Federation only recently. This will be the first election in which it has taken part. Their admission to the Federation was vigorously opposed by the Achernarian planets. It is the Achernarians who represent the greatest threat to us in the coming election."

"So I'm to pull political chestnuts out of the fire for you?"

"In a way. There is an Acruxian agent on Regulus and we have no idea what he is planning in the way of sabotage. But Regulus has very lax laws about political candidates and the Acruxian agent is also running for the office of Senator from Regulus. As an independent. Because of opposition to Regulus, the only other candidate for the office is a Republocrat. A native named Xelia Zon. In order to defeat the Acruxian, you may have to do something which will help the Republocrat candidate."

MANNING FROWNED. "So that's why you can't use the cops," he said. "It's illegal for any government official, in that capacity, to help one candidate over another."

"That's it," J. Barnaby admitted. "If we used the police, it might provide the Achernarians with enough ammunition to defeat us. On the other hand, if we do nothing, the Acruxian agent may succeed in throwing us into war—either civil war or war with Acrux. That leaves it up to you, Manning."

"Okay. Do I have any kind of authority, or do I go merely as a nosy citizen?"

"I've arranged for you to go as an election observer for the Republocrat Party. That's about the best I could do."

"Great," Manning said dryly. "Do you have any other helpful little hints?"

"Just a reminder that it's only a couple of days until elections," J. Barnaby said briskly. "I'll expect you to have the whole thing cleaned up before then. And, Manning…"

"Yes?"

"When you've got the problem whipped into shape, if you can think of some way to give the solution wide publicity, it would be appreciated."

"You don't happen to have a short-handled star-duster, do you?" Manning asked. "We could tie it on the back of my ship and I could dust off a few stars while I'm doing the other things. I wouldn't want you to think I have too much spare time on my hands."

"I'll even laugh at your jokes," J. Barnaby said sourly, "if you clear this up for us. Now, if you'll excuse me, Manning, I have an appointment with the Ambassador from Altair…."

"And I remember when you only had appointments with people who wanted to buy life insurance," Manning murmured. He stood up. "Okay, father-in-law. Hold on to your striped pants." He turned and left the office.

As soon as he reached the spaceport, he blasted off. Once he was above the planet, he fed the co-ordinates of Regulus II into the automatic pilot and put the ship into magnidrive. Then he dug out an encyclotape on Acruxians and leaned back to listen to it. He could learn about Regulus when he got there, but he had a hunch he'd better find out about Acruxians before he tangled with one.

CHAPTER TWO

THE *ALPHA ACTUARY* came out of magnidrive and dropped slowly down toward the surface of Regulus II. Manning Draco stared at the landing screen and wondered if someone had been kidding him. On the entire planet there was only one building in sight and it was a modest dwelling no larger than the average mansion anywhere in the Federation. It certainly wasn't large enough to hold the population of a planet. Besides, its architecture was pure Terran.

There was a small spaceport near the single house and Manning set his ship down on it. He cut the power and threw open the air-lock.

There were two individuals waiting for him as he climbed out of the ship. The first was a Terran, a tall, austere man wearing the formal garb which was still so dear to the hearts of Terran politicians. His welcome was anything but warm.

"I suppose," he said, offering a limp handshake, "you're this Manning Draco person I was told to expect? The election observer, or some such thing?"

"Some such thing," Manning said, returning the handshake.

"Can't imagine why they send anyone—even an observer— to this miserable place," the man said, making no effort to lower his voice. "You're aware, of course, that I'm the Terran Ambassador?"

"I guessed it," Manning said dryly. "It was hard work, but I did it."

The Ambassador stared blankly back at him. "The Secretary of Planets telephoned me you were coming. I don't suppose he sent any word on my request to be transferred?"

"No."

The Ambassador sighed heavily. "Perhaps if I made a larger contribution," he murmured. "Is there anything I can do for you, Mr.—ah— what was your name?"

"Don't even try to remember it," Manning said. "I wouldn't want you to suffer any mental strain. Now, you just run along."

"I suppose this—ah— native is waiting to see you," the Ambassador said. He sniffed audibly. "Well, I really must be getting back." He turned and trotted rapidly in the direction of the house.

Manning grinned as he saw him go, then turned for his first look at a Regulusian.

The creature who faced him stood upright and was almost as tall as Manning. He wore a one-piece suit roughly similar to those worn by Terrans, although it was cut in the back to accommodate a long, round tail which was covered with short, silky hair. His hands, although still bearing a resemblance to paws, were very human-like and were also covered with silky fur. His face was rather pointed, with a receding forehead. The nose was by far the most prominent feature. Not only was it long, but on the very tip of it there were twenty-two light-pink fleshy fingers growing in the form of a star.[1]

"Hello," Manning said. "I'm Manning Draco. Are you here to meet me?"

"Yes," said the Regulusian, finally advancing. As he continued to speak, Manning noticed that he spoke Terran with almost no accent. "I would have introduced myself sooner, but your Ambassador is fond of the formal approach—through channels—and I did not wish to anger him. I am Xelia Zon, Mr. Draco."

"Call me Manning. I'm glad to know you, Xelia." He put out his hand and was somewhat surprised to find that the Regulusian had whipped his tail around and coiled it about his hand.

---

1   Primitive Regulusians had been closely related to the Terran family *Talpidae,* species *Condylura cristata,* sometimes known as the Star-Nosed Mole. Present-day Regutlusians are, however, as far advanced over their ancestors as Terrans are over *Pithecantropus erectus.*

"I see you are surprised," said the Regulusian. "This is your first trip to Regulus?"

Manning admitted that it was.

"So few of your people come here," Xelia Zon said. "Like you Terrans, we have the custom of establishing a physical contact on being introduced. You do this by shaking hands; we do it by shaking tails. I imagine that this developed because the tail is an important sense organ to us."

"Sounds logical," Manning said. By this time he was so accustomed to the many differences through the Galaxy that he seldom thought twice about any of them.

"I believe it is one of the things which disturbs your Terran Ambassador. In fact, he was heard saying that he disliked suddenly finding a tail in his hand."

"Nothing could be worse than that limp hand he offers," Manning said with a grin. "You know why I'm here?"

"To observe our election. Or so I was informed by the chairman of the party. I'm afraid there will be little to observe."

"If you're Xelia Zon," Manning said, "then you must be the candidate for Senator."

"I was," Xelia Zon said ruefully. "As of the moment, however, the party has no candidate for the Senate. That's why I say there will be little for you to observe. I was almost hoping that the party might decide to send some sort of Federation policeman, but I suppose that was out of the question."

"The Acruxian?" Manning asked.

"The Acruxian," Xelia said, nodding. "I'll tell you all about it, but why not wait until we reach your room. I took the liberty of making a reservation for you at our best hotel. Shall we go?"

"Where?" Manning asked. He looked around again at the sparsely shrubbed, flat ground. "I meant to ask you about your cities. I thought I saw both sides of the planet as I came in, but I didn't see anything that looked like a city, or even a village."

The Regulusian smiled, showing even, pointed teeth. "You are standing directly over our capital city right now."

Manning lifted one foot and looked down. "Dehydrated?" he asked.

Xelia Zon laughed. "Hardly. Come. I'll show you."

HE LED the way around the *Alpha Actuary* and toward a small kiosk which Manning had not previously noticed. They entered the kiosk and walked down a few steps and then into an elevator. The door closed as soon as they were in it and they lunged smoothly downward.

"Underground, eh?" Manning said. "All of your cities?"

Xelia Zon nodded. "Not only our cities, but also our farms, and every other part of our civilization."

"Protection?"

"Perhaps. More likely, tradition. We are evolved from a race which carried on its life beneath the surface of the ground, so I suppose we feel more comfortable there. Then, by now, there are many advantages. For example, we are able to get twice the yield on crops that we would on the surface."

"How? I should think the lack of sunlight…."

"We plant on both the floor and the ceiling of the underground farm. As for sunlight, we grow many crops that don't require it at all, and for those that do we have methods of piping sunlight in underground—do you find the idea of living underground unpleasant?"

"Why should I?" Manning asked, shrugging. "Then that one house on the surface is our Ambassador's?"

"Yes. He flatly refused to live in Zeloha, the city to which we are going. The Ambassadors from the other Federation planets are all living in the city, although I suspect that some of them don't relish it either. You wonder, perhaps, why I tell you this?"

"I imagine you have your reasons," Manning said, "and when you're ready you'll tell them to me."

Xelia Zon nodded and the tiny fingers of the star on his nose flushed a darker pink.[2] "It is related to the reason you're here," he said. "I shall soon explain the connection."

The elevator stopped and the door slid noiselessly open. Manning followed Xelia Zon out onto a broad strip of concrete, brightly illumined by indirect lighting. Near the exit, there was a long, streamlined vehicle which Manning guessed was a Regulusian car. This turned out to be correct, for Xelia led the way directly to it and they climbed in. Xelia pressed a number of buttons and the car leaped forward. Manning could feel the pull of a powerful motor, but there was practically no sound.

Xelia turned the car into a broad street and they picked up speed. After a while, they began to see other cars on the street.

Within a few minutes they had reached the edge of the city. There were a number of buildings on either side which looked as if they might be stores. Most of the signs were in an unfamiliar script which Manning assumed was Regulusian, although there were a few in Terran and other Federation languages. The buildings were all only one story high, and the architecture mostly looked like the upper half of an egg.

"I suppose," Manning said, "that one of the penalties of building underground is that you're restricted on how high you can make your buildings. Doesn't that make the city take up a lot of space?"

Xelia Zon grinned. "I'm afraid you're still thinking in terms of Terran culture. These buildings are all of fifteen or twenty stories and we have many that are still larger. You see, here, the street floor is the top one. Everything is built toward the core of our planet instead of skyward, as you build."

"I'm beginning to get it," Manning said. "Everything works just the opposite as with us." He grinned. "Tell me, is it true what they say about Regulusian women—" He broke off as he realized Xelia Zon wasn't getting it. "Never mind. It wasn't even a very good joke when it first started on Terra a long time ago."

---

2   Whenever a Regulusian is pleased his nose blushes. Since the Regulusians are the least meddlesome race in the Galaxy, this led to Professor Horatio Schlemozel offering the facetious explanation that the Regulusians' noses blushed with pride because they weren't being thrust into anybody else's business.

"If you'll notice," Xelia said, "you'll see the burrow-ways running off the street and leading down to the last floor, which is usually used for parking."

Manning saw the openings, looking like tunnels, angling down from each side of the street.

BY THIS TIME traffic was fairly heavy and there were considerable numbers of Regulusians on the sidewalks hurrying about their business. Considering the size of the city, there were very few citizens from other planets.

Everywhere the street was bright with the same indirect lighting Manning had noticed earlier, but once they passed through a section where the quality of light was different, more like sunlight.

"It is sunlight," Xelia said when Manning asked him about it. "This is one of the sections to which we pipe sunlight from the surface. Most of the embassies from other planets are in this section and it is done here for their convenience."

Finally Xelia's car darted into one of the burrow-ways and began the descent. When he braked the car to a stop, they were obviously inside a building. There were a number of other cars parked on the floor.

"This," Xelia said, answering the expression on Manning's face before he could put it into words, "is the top floor—you would call it the bottom floor—of the hotel where you will stay." He opened the car door and stepped out.

Manning followed him. "By the way," he said casually, "are the Regulusians telepathic?"

Xelia Zon looked at him in surprise, then laughed. "Oh—you ask because I answered your question before you asked it? We Regulusians are very sensitive to expressions and attitudes. Quite often I have a good idea of what you're going to say just before you speak. But that's all. As you probably know, there aren't many telepathic races. The Martians, Rigelians, Sabikians, I believe, and Acruxians. Like many of the nontelepathic races, we Regulusians have natural barriers to telepathic readings."

Manning had already discovered this, but he only nodded as they entered an elevator.

"I've heard," Xelia continued, "that there is at least one Terran who is not only telepathic, but also has developed a secondary mind-shield, which is quite rare even among telepathic races. But, of course, this may be one of those rumors that get around."

Manning didn't bother to tell him that he was the one Terran who possessed this unusual mental equipment. He was certain that the Regulusian was trustworthy, but there was no point in taking chances. He had already learned that Acruxians were telepaths; if the Acruxian agent who was on Regulus didn't learn of Manning's unique ability, it might one day prove a slight advantage.

They stopped on the next floor and confirmed the reservation. Again, as they passed through the lobby, Manning saw that nearly everyone there was a Regulusian. He did catch sight of a couple of Vegans, a Capellan, and a Polluxian who was obviously a traveling salesman, but it was a small number of non-natives for such a large city.

Again they took an elevator. "This, at least," said Manning as the elevator surged upward, "is a familiar sensation. We're going *up* to reach the room."

"Actually," said Xelia with a smile, "we are going down, since we entered what we call the top floor."

"I've often been accused of not knowing down from up," Manning said dryly, "but this is the first time it's ever been proved."

XELIA CHUCKLED as the elevator stopped. They followed the Regulusian bellhop down the corridor to a room. It was, Manning saw as soon as they entered, completely equipped for Terrans. This was not unusual in the Galaxy, but what was unusual in such a modern city was that Manning had not seen another Terran since they'd left the Ambassador on the surface. He commented on this to Xelia.

"Yes," Xelia said soberly. "We have provided many typically

Terran conveniences, but very few of your race ever come here. Those who do mostly react the way your Ambassador did. Would you care to join me in a drink? We also have Terran beverages."

"I'll have whatever you're having," Manning said. He was always inclined to try native drinks despite a couple of bad experiences. Once, on Praesepe I, it had taken two days to recover his voice after such an adventure.

Xelia ordered the drinks over a plain audiophone attached to the wall of the room.

"No visiphone?" Manning asked.

Xelia shook his head. "We have no visicasts at all. I suppose that eventually we'll be getting sets since the Federation visicasts will now be beamed to us, but we Regulusians have always preferred actually being present at our entertainment instead of watching some reproduction of it." He smiled slightly. "We are, of course, considered backward because of this and because we have never tried to develop space flight."

A light blinked on the wall and a panel slid open, revealing their drinks. Xelia took the two glasses and handed one to Manning. It was filled with a cloudy purple liquid which was rather horrible to look at but which, Manning discovered, tasted very pleasant. He sipped the drink and waited for Xelia to speak.

"Since you've never been to Regulus," Xelia said finally, "I should like to explain something about my people. It has a bearing on the election and the Acruxian. As you know, our admission to the Federation was opposed by many, especially the Achemarians. Their feeling is based on the fact that Achernarians are evolved from various forms of insect life and there was a time when primitive Regulusians ate insects. That was, however, many generations ago. The Achernarians of today are quite different from the insects my ancestors found so delectable, and we have also changed. The protein life which we still eat has been carefully bred from a type of insect found only on Regulus. It is not an intelligent form of life and might be compared to the cattle you Terrans have bred for food."

Manning nodded. As an insurance investigator, he had traveled over enough of the Galaxy to be familiar with the many prejudices that existed. "The Achernarians have sent an Ambassador here, haven't they?" he asked.

"Yes. No one ever sees him, but he's here. Now, Manning, you see we are hated and feared by a number of life forms in the Federation. Then you Terrans—I hope you will forgive me if I speak frankly—are inclined to view us with something like contempt. The attitude of your Ambassador is an excellent example. I don't find this attitude in you, Manning, but it is what we've come to expect from most Terrans. As a result, there is a lot of anti-Terran, even anti-human, feeling on Regulus, as well as considerable anti-Federation propaganda."

"Understandable," said Manning. "In fact, it's not even peculiar to Regulus."

AT THIS Xelia nodded. "I was one of of the leaders of the movement which led to Regulus joining the Federation. Not because I believe in accepting the way we're treated, but because I believe it is necessary for our own safety. I therefore favor cooperation, without accepting submission. Because of this, I have long been an object of attack from the anti-Terran and anti-Federation forces. Which brings us to the election. I was, as you know, the Republocratic candidate for Senator from Regulus. The other political parties did not nominate candidates here and I was the only one running until Dtilla Raishelle declared himself an independent candidate."

"Dtilla Raishelle? The Acruxian?"

Xelia nodded.

"Tell me one thing," Manning said. "How is it possible for an Acruxian to run for a Regulusian office? Acruxis is not even a part of the Federation."

"True," Xelia said. "We, however, still have many antiquated laws on our statute books. In the old days, no one from other planets ever came to Regulus. So our laws state that anyone who owns property on Regulus is considered a citizen and may run for political office. Dtilla Raishelle bought a house when he arrived here a month ago."

"And he is backed by the anti-Terran movement?"

"Completely. His platform is entirely anti-Terran and anti-Achernarian. From the beginning he had such strong support that I knew it would be difficult for me to win. Now it is impossible."

"What do you mean?"

"I am no longer a candidate," Xelia said bitterly. His nose had faded to a pale pink which was almost white. "More of our ancient laws. Seldom enforced, we have laws which compel candidates to submit to various physical tests such as walking tightropes, juggling, and sleight-of-hand. It is also permitted for a candidate to challenge an opposing candidate to any sort of a personal test, or duel. When this happens, the loser, if still alive, must automatically withdraw from the political race. There is no choice. You cannot refuse the challenge and a loser cannot remain a candidate."

"The Acruxian challenged you to a duel?"

"If you know anything about Acruxians, you know of their fabulous strength. I had no chance. The duel was held last night in the Shaun Arena. Dtilla Raishelle is now the only candidate for Regulusian Senator."

"Can't the Republocrats nominate another candidate?"

"No. It would make no difference if we could. I'm sure no one would agree to run—otherwise they could declare themselves an independent. Besides, there is no Regulusian who is a match for an Acruxian and there would merely be another challenge. That's why I said there would be little for you to observe."

The more he heard, the more Manning Draco wished he were back in his own office with nothing more complex to worry about than the vacation problems of a honeymooning threesome from Sirius. "There is a feeling on Terra," he said slowly, "that this Acruxian may have more in mind than merely running for office. As a Senator from Regulus, he could be a nuisance, but that is all. Do you think he might have something else in mind?"

"I'm sure of it," Xelia said firmly, "but I have no idea what it is, I was suspicious of him when he first arrived. I asked our Central Security to give me complete reports on his movements. There is nothing in those reports which mean anything—unless he and the Achernarians are planning something together."

"Why he and the Achernarians?" Manning asked.

"Since arriving here, he has made a number of speeches and has attended parties which were held for political purposes. These are normal activities for a candidate. But he has also paid three visits to the Achernarian Ambassador."

"Okay," Manning said. "I think I'd like to meet this Acruxian."

"That's easily arranged," Xelia said. His tone indicated that he didn't think the meeting, or anything else, would accomplish much. "There's a political party tonight—to celebrate the Acruxian's forthcoming victory, as a matter of fact. You can go as my guest."

"Good," said Manning. He finished his drink. "After I've looked him over, I'd like to see the reports you had on him. Maybe we can figure out something. In the meantime, if you don't mind, I think I'll rest."

"Certainly," said Xelia, standing up. "I shall pick you up in about three hours. I trust you will rest well." He offered his tail for a brief shaking, then left. It was obvious that he liked Manning personally but had given up expecting anything that would help the situation.

Manning stretched out on the bed and went to sleep. He had a hunch that there might be little sleep between now and the election and he might as well get what he could.

CHAPTER THREE

MANNING DRACO was waiting in the hotel room when Xelia Zon came back that evening. He had awakened earlier and had dinner in his room so that he was ready to go. They went down (Xelia insisted it was up) and climbed into the Regulusian's car.

After a short drive through the city streets, Xelia stopped before an ornate private home. A formally attired Regulusian butler met them at the door and conducted them to the elevator. They dropped down some ten floors, where they were met by another servant. He led them through a number of well-appointed rooms and out into a splendid underground garden. It was filled with strange, beautiful flowers and shrubs and had piped-in sunlight

The party was well under way, the guests being almost exclusively Regulusians. While he was not openly insulted, it soon became obvious that most of those present were anti-Terran.

There were only a few who were friends of Xelia and were consequently friendly toward him.

Almost as soon as they'd entered the garden, Manning had noticed a group at one end of the garden. There was a creature in the center of the group, towering over them, who was undoubtedly the Acruxian. He guessed that Xelia had also caught sight of them, for they were slowly working toward that end of the garden.

They had just stopped a passing servant and snared two drinks from his tray, and were walking on toward the one group, when Manning felt a hand on his arm. "Well," said a husky voice, "this is a pleasant surprise."

Manning looked around, then did a double-take. At first glance, he thought she was a Terran. It was only when he looked much closer than he realized her head was covered with silky blond fur instead of hair. But that was the only way in which she differed from a Terran girl. She had all the other Terran feminine attributes, in the right places and in the right amounts, adding up to one of the most beautiful creatures he had ever seen. Her figure was one which would make any man glad that the styles of 3473 featured a great deal of exposed skin.

"Hello," he said. "Do I know you?"

"No, but you will," she said. Her voice had those husky tones that for many centuries had sent shivers running down the spines of Terran males. Her eyes, great golden orbs, seemed to contain the same quality—a nameless yearning to which men were drawn in the hope that they could satisfy it. "I had almost given up hope of seeing a fellow humanoid on this planet when you walked in."

"Fellow humanoid?" Manning said.

She laughed, her voice like sensual music. "I can hardly say a fellow human, can I? I'm not human, you know."

Manning was trying to place her. There were a number of humanoid races throughout the Federation, notably the Martians and the Muphridians. They were remarkably like the humans of Terra, although their origins were usually quite different, although there was nearly always some one difference. Quite often, it was the hair. The Muphridians, for example, had feathers in place of hair. He was sure that this girl was from none of the places he had visited.

In the meantime, the girl was speaking again. "Xelia Zon," she was saying, "the least you can do is introduce me to your charming Terran friend."

"Manning," Xelia said, not especially happily, "this is Velmar Shonda. Manning Draco."

"What a lovely name," exclaimed the girl. "I may call you Manning, may I not?"

"You may," Manning said. "Where are you from? I don't think I've ever met anyone who looked exactly like you."

"I'm from Aldebaran. But from the *third* planet in the system, if you please."

Manning had the feeling that there was something about the Aldebaranese that he should know, but it eluded him. He wondered what she was doing on Regulus and if it had any bearing on the reason he was there. He glanced at Xelia Zon, who must have seen the question in his face.

"I don't know what she's doing here," he said, shrugging his shoulders. "She has been here for about two months, I understand, although this is only the fourth or fifth time I've seen her."

THE GIRL from Aldebaran laughed again. "Your Regulusian friend doesn't like me," she said. She managed somehow to make "Regulusian" sound like an unflattering word. "That is why he is so blunt, Manning. But I am here on a visit, just as you are. I came intending to stay only a few days, but the natives are so quaint I've stayed longer. I am what you Terrans call an anthropologist. It has been rather lonely, of course—but I can see that won't be true after tonight."

Marriage had worked several changes in Manning Draco. He loved Vega and liked being married to her. He had every intention of remaining faithful to her, not because the Terran tradition was as strong as it had once been but because he believed that a life with her could be complete. At the same time, he was a normal enough man to be flattered by Velmar's attitude and to have a certain amount of response to it.

"By the way," she said, "have you met the Acruxian who is here? Dtilla Raishelle?"

"We were just on our way to meet him," Manning said.

"Oh, let me introduce you," she said, urging him forward with her hand on his arm. "He is such a fascinating character."

"I can hardly wait," Manning said dryly. But he went forward under her urging and Xelia Zon kept pace with them.

As they neared the group which contained the Acruxian, Manning Draco controlled that part of his mind which worked in front of the secondary shield, so that it would seem that he was nothing more than another curious Terran. He knew that the Acruxian would probably try a brief mental probe and if his first response was no more than that he would probe no farther and so would not discover the secondary shield.

Velmar Shonda cleared a way through the little group until they stood in front of the Acruxian. "Manning," she said, "I'd like you to meet the distinguished Regulusian candidate for the Assembly of the Stars, the future Senator from Regulus, Dtilla Raishelle. Senator Dtilla, this is Manning Draco of Terra."

As he'd expected, Manning felt the mental power of the Acruxian nibble briefly at his thoughts. Then, apparently satisfied, it withdrew.

"I am deeply honored," the Acruxian said in a booming voice, extending a tentacle. Like all Acruxians, he had difficulty in pronouncing the letter *r*, but otherwise his Terran was impeccable.

"The pleasure is all mine," returned Manning. He reached out and grasped the proffered tentacle, immediately raising his hand high in the air in the Acruxian manner of shaking hands (or shaking tentacles, to be exact).

"Ah," said the Acruxian, "you are familiar with the customs of my people?"

"Only to a small degree," Manning said modestly, not bothering to add that he had learned all he knew that afternoon from an encyclotape and this was the first time he had ever seen anyone from Acrux.

Dtilla Raishelle was a typical Acruxian. He stood seven feet tall, his huge cylindrical body supported on three sturdy legs. His body was dark gray in color and was bare except for a dark green fringed skirt, which was an Acruxian ceremonial dress. A holster, attached to the skirt, held a ceremonial tri-blast.[3] His head was a round knob, pale red, perfectly smooth except for a mouth opening and inverted ears which were covered by fine, sensitive hairs. He had four tentacles, two at waist level and two at shoulder level. Two eye-stalks reared several inches above his head.[4]

---

3   The tri-blast was a three-barrelled blade-gun peculiar to Acrux. It was used in all ceremonial duels and was designed to amputate all three legs of the opponent.
4   Although, as this description shows, somewhat of a sport model, Acruxians are related to Rigelians. As more ancient readers will recognize, Dtilla Raishelle

AT THE MOMENT, the eye-stalks were sharply inclined toward Manning and there was an expression of suspicion in them. As the Acruxian very well knew, few ordinary Terrans knew anything about Acruxians. It had been many generations since anything but a merciless cold war had existed between Acrux and its satellites and the more dominant planets of the Federation.

At this moment, Manning spoke a few words in the quick, liquid Acruxian language—a ceremonial greeting of respect which he had learned that afternoon from a linguatape.

"You speak my language, too," Dtilla Raishelle exclaimed. His voice indicated pleasure, but the suspicion in his eyes deepened.

"Just that one sentence," Manning said. "My father was once space-wrecked near your home and I guess he picked up those few things which he taught me."

Once more he felt the Acruxian probe his surface thought, but he was prepared for it and the memory there was just as he said. The Acruxian suddenly relaxed, although there was still a touch of suspicion in his eyes. Just enough, Manning hoped. He didn't want to precipitate a contest with the Acruxian, but he did want him to be enough off guard so that he might later make a move which would help trap him.

It was then that Manning noticed the unusually large piece of luggage which sat on the ground beside Dtilla's feet. It was at least three and a half feet long and probably two feet high. It was made of some shining metallic plastic. There were tentacle-loops along the top for easy carrying.

"What's that?" Manning asked. "You're not leaving, are you—just when everyone says your election is a sure thing?"

"No," Dtilla Raishelle said. He hesitated and Manning could

---

was, therefore, a distant cousin of Dzanku Dzanku, the Rigelian who was for so long the deadly enemy of Manning Draco. It had taken Manning a full year to best Dzanku and get rid of him in a Time-Fracture which made it impossible for Dzanku to return short of a century.

guess that he was trying to decide what sort of answer would be believed. Manning would have liked to try a swift mental probe, but knew it might be a serious mistake. Still, without even trying, he could feel mental waves of hatred which must be coming from the Acruxian. He was sure they weren't coming from the Regulusians or the Aldebaranese—he'd already discovered that she had a natural shield to telepathy. That left only Dtilla, unless—he quickly suppressed the thought for fear the Acruxian might catch it.

"This," Dtilla continued, indicating the box, "contains many of the rare, delicate perfumes of my home planet. I believe they are too subtle for most other life forms, but they help to make my stay away from home more comfortable." His eye-stalks turned to survey the Regulusians. "I don't believe that I ever offered the Retails to you, my friends, having only told you that it was a custom of my people. I am sorry if my previous reticence has offended you in any way."

"No, no," exclaimed several Regulusians.

"Well," Manning said, "we mustn't interrupt your conversation with your friends any longer—"

"Think nothing of it," Dtilla Raishelle said, waving his tentacles. It was obvious that he was still mildly curious about Manning. "I have not seen many Terrans here. Are you on a business trip?"

Even as he was speaking, Manning decided to answer with part of the truth. He believed that he had convinced the Acruxian that he was a fairly ordinary Terran; now it was time to let him know that even so he might be an enemy.

"In a way," Manning said. "I'm here for the elections. As an observer—although I don't suppose there will be much to observe."

"An observer, eh? But not to interfere, I hope. I believe that is illegal."

"I wouldn't think of interfering," Manning said. "I shall probably sit on the sidelines and hope that the best man wins."

"Inasmuch as I am the only remaining candidate in the Senatorial race," the Acruxian said, and his amusement was evident in the agitation of his eye-stalks, "I believe the identity of the best—er—man is a foregone conclusion."

"Maybe," Manning said. "But there's an old Terran proverb—which I just invented—that says there's many an obstacle between the loot and the tentacle. Now, if you'll excuse me, I'd like to devote more of my time to this young lady."

Pulling Velmar Shonda with him, Manning Draco walked away, conscious that the Acruxian was watching him with renewed interest.

"I salute your going away," Dtilla Raishelle called after him.[5]

As they left the Acruxian, Xelia Zon joined another group of Regulusians, while Manning and Velmar walked on and sat down beneath one of the umbrella-like shrubs.

"You shouldn't have been so hard on Dtilla," Velmar said. "He's really a fascinating creature and terribly brilliant and talented."

"I don't doubt it," Manning said. "Why are you defending him? Are you his girlfriend?"

"Goodness, no," Velmar Shonda said, laughing. "I admire creatures like Dtilla and I confess I find his mind very stimulating. But that's all. We Aldebaranese are—constructed very much like Terrans and when it comes to the more intimate relationships in life, I much prefer a handsome Terran—like you."

This was a new experience for Manning. In the past, he had always met such advances more than halfway. He knew what to do when a woman said no; he'd never learned how to say no himself.

"I—I'm married," he said defensively.

---

5 This was only an approximate translation of the Acruxian expression Dtilla had in mind. In the original, it was one of those double-meaning phrases so common to Acrux in which Dtilla was saying goodby and at the same time implying that Manning was leaving because he recognized his own inferior status. Dr. Homer Aybar, who has compiled the only *Dictionary of Acruxian Idioms*, speaks of such phrases as "the insult elegant."

"I like married men," Velmar Shonda declared. "Then, too, they are not so apt to become all squishy if there's a slight accident, and insist on marrying you."

"Er—" said Manning, which was not a brilliant beginning, but was all he could think of at the moment. Fortunately, he didn't have to think any further, for Xelia Zon arrived at that moment.

"I'm sorry," he said politely, "but I think we'd better leave, Manning. You remember you wanted to make one other stop before we returned to the hotel."

"Of course," Manning exclaimed. He got to his feet, relieved, and his aplomb returned with the rescue. He looked down and grinned at the Aldebaranese. "I'm sorry, honey, but I have to run along. I'll see you soon."

"Sooner than you expect," she answered, and it seemed that the strange hunger in her eyes was stronger. "Goodby—for now."

CHAPTER FOUR

AT THE OFFICES of the Regulusian Central Security, Xelia Zon spoke to an official who was also a friend of his and a few minutes later they were in a small room with the complete reports on Dtilla Raishelle. Manning read them rapidly but thoroughly.

"What's this?" he asked, stopping with a finger pointing to one paragraph. "Something about Dtilla and the missing Regulusians."

"It was a false lead," Xelia said, "For a time, they thought they had something on the Acruxian, but it didn't work out."

"But what was it?" Manning insisted.

"A strange thing," said Xelia, frowning. "During the past six weeks or so a number of Regulusians—ten of them, to be exact—have vanished mysteriously. No trace of them has been found at all. At first, it was thought that perhaps the Acruxian had murdered them, but then some of them vanished at times when he couldn't possibly have had anything to do with them."

"Maybe they were just murdered," Manning murmured, going back to reading the reports.

"Not unless they were murdered by outsiders," Xelia said. "We have no crime of any sort on Regulus. There has never been a murder committed by a Regulusian in the history of our race."

"Really?" Manning said, momentarily interested. "No wonder you have trouble fitting into the Federation." He bent over the reports again.

There was nothing in them that Xelia hadn't already told him. Dtilla Raishelle had made speeches and gone to political parties and he had made three visits to the Achernarian Ambassador. The rest of the time he had stayed in the house he'd purchased.

"I had hoped," Manning said as they handed the reports back, "that I'd find some reference to that piece of luggage Dtilla had with him tonight. I wonder if he carries it with him every time he goes out."

"He's had it every time I've seen him, but that doesn't cover all his activities," Xelia said. He looked at his friend, the official.

"The ones who made these reports," the official said, "are not on duty tonight. You might return tomorrow and ask them, if you like."

Manning nodded and turned away. Xelia Zon joined him and they left the building.

"Why are you so interested in the Acruxian's luggage?" Xelia asked.

"Because he was lying about why he had it with him," Manning said. "I'm sure of that. I think he offered a story which he thought I would be willing to accept. Therefore, the luggage must in some way be important to his scheme, whatever it is."

"If you think it important," Xelia said, "perhaps we could trick him away from it long enough to let a Central Security locksmith get at it. We have some clever ones."

"Pick the lock, Xelia? I thought you Regulusians knew nothing about crime."

"It would be no crime, done by an official in the name of Security," Xelia explained. "Shall we try it?"

Manning shook his head. "It would only make him step up his schedule if it failed—and I'm sure it would. I believe that your locksmiths are clever, but I understand that Acruxians have a way with locks which is unmatched in the universe. They have a small tendril on one tentacle which permits them to read any lock. Not only can they pick locks anywhere, but they are able to build such intricate locks that they defy picking by anyone else."

Xelia was silent until they had almost reached the hotel. He seemed embarrassed when he finally did speak.

"I like you, Manning," he said, "so I hesitate to mention this—but aren't you exceeding your authority as a political observer? I know there are stiff penalties for interfering in any way with an election—which is what Dtilla Raishelle might claim—and I'd hate to see you get in trouble."

"Thanks, Xelia," Manning said. "No, I'm not exceeding it yet. As of this moment, I'm just curious and *that* hasn't as yet been outlawed. But I would like to know what our Acruxian is up to."

"So would I," murmured Xelia.

THEY ARRIVED at the hotel and started through the lobby. They were almost to the elevator when they heard the desk clerk calling:

"Mr. Draco," the clerk said, "there was someone here to see you. It was rather peculiar—he insisted on asking all sorts of questions as to where you were and when you'd be back, but I could have sworn that he wasn't really listening to my answers. Even so, I had quite a time getting rid of him."

"Did he leave his name?" Manning asked.

The clerk nodded. "Chaun Cla, of this city. He said that he would call again."

Manning looked at Xelia. The latter nodded. "I know the name. He is one of those who has been supporting Dtilla Raishelle and was with him there in the garden tonight."

Manning grinned. "I thought we might expect something. Dtilla doesn't think I represent much of a threat, but he doesn't want to take any chances. They're up to something.'"

"Should I call my friend at Central Security and ask him to keep a check on Chaun Cla?"

"It might be a good idea," said Manning. "I'll go on up to the room. Come up when you're through."

"I'll come *down* when I'm through," Xelia said with a grin.

Manning laughed and went to the elevator. Arriving on his floor, he went down the corridor keeping a careful watch, but he saw nothing out of order. He listened at the door of his room for a minute, but heard nothing. There was some faint exotic perfume in the corridor. He unlocked his door and went in. Velmar Shonda, the Aldebaranese beauty, was sitting in the room, amusement in her golden eyes.

"Hello, Manning," she said huskily. "I told you I'd see you sooner than you expected."

"How did you get in here?" Manning asked.

She shrugged. "One of the bellhops. They are susceptible to feminine wiles and money. I used both."

She stood up and came close to him. Her perfume washed over him like waves of desire.

"Manning," she said softly, "I know that most Terran men like their females to be receptive rather than aggressive. But I have no patience for the tricks of Terran females. I like you—why shouldn't I say so? I have been here two months without any male of my kind—"

She leaned, closer to him, her breasts almost brushing his chest. Her parted lips were a deep red and he could glimpse the white teeth between them. Her eyes were like melting gold—plus that something else which was almost familiar, but not quite.

"Manning—" she said, knowing that he understood and that the rest didn't have to be said.

ALTHOUGH HE NEVER admitted it to anyone but himself, it was a struggle. If Xelia hadn't been coming to the room, Manning knew that he might not have had the peculiar strength that it needed to shake his head at what was being offered.

"Honey," he said as lightly as he could, "you're a beautiful hunk of woman. Maybe you're in the right room, but it's the wrong time. My friend will be here any minute."

"Send him away," she said.

"I can't," Manning answered and the regret in his voice wasn't all pretended. "It's important. He and I have to talk."

She pouted and her yellow eyes seemed to get larger.

"There'll be other times, honey," he said. He didn't know whether he meant it or not; he did know that he had a feeling that it would be a mistake to make an enemy of her.

She straightened up and looked at him curiously. "There have not been many men who shook their heads at Velmar Shonda," she said. Then she shrugged and some part of the amusement returned to her eyes. "As you say, for now. But do not keep me waiting too long, Manning."

She was gone, leaving the room so silently that he was almost unaware of her going. But the air of the room was still heavy with her scent. Manning dropped heavily into the chair and loosened the collar of his one-piece suit.

"Whew," he said.

The scent was still strong in the room when Xelia Zon arrived. Manning saw the fingers of his nose twitch[6] but he made no reference to the perfume.

"My friend will see that the activities of Chaun Cla are checked," he said.

---

6 There was considerable misunderstanding between Terrans and Regulusians when they first met. For a long time the Terrans thought that every Regulusian they met was thumbing his nose at them.

Manning nodded. "Okay," he said. He grinned at the Regulusian. "I guess I ought to make arrangements for you to chaperone me day and night while I'm here. It might be safer."

Xelia Zon pretended to first notice the scent of perfume. "Velmar Shonda?" he asked.

"In person," said Manning. "Just being in the same room with her is like a postgraduate course in seduction. If she's a fair example, no wonder Aldebaran industry is so far behind the rest of the Federation."

"I am not familiar with the Aldebaran civilization," Xelia said solemnly, but there was a discernible twinkle an his eyes.

"There's very little exchange between Aldebaran and the rest of the Federation and I'm beginning to understand why," Manning said. His face grew thoughtful. "You know, Xelia, the actions of Chaun Cla were like a delaying tactic. Do you suppose it was to help her get into my room? Could she be working for Dtilla Raishelle?"

"She might be. I believe that she has been very friendly with the Acruxian. And they did arrive here at about the same time."

"I thought of that," Manning said. "Still, why go through all that business with the desk clerk? She said that she bribed a bellhop to let her in and I think she was telling the truth. Maybe she is working for Dtilla, but Chaun Cla must have been covering up for something else." He was silent a moment, then got to his feet.

"I've just thought of something," he said quietly. "Maybe it was a three-way job. Velmar Shonda was in my room when I arrived. I assure you that was enough to keep me from thinking about anything else. Maybe that was the point."

"What do you mean?"

"Let's search the room. And be careful, Xelia. There are some nasty species in the Galaxy and some of them may be concealed in here."

THEY COVERED every inch of the room without finding anything that shouldn't have been there. Although he hadn't

been aware of working faster than usual, Manning was breath-
ing hard and there was a strange ringing in his ears as he dropped
into a chair.

"Nothing," he said. "I don't get it."

"Maybe—maybe—" Xelia Zon seemed to be having trouble
getting his words out and he was clawing at his neck.

As he watched the Regulusian, Manning realized that his own
breath was getting shorter instead of improving now that he was
resting. He struggled to his feet and crossed the room. The effort
was almost too much, but he made it to the door and flung it
open. He could almost feel the air pressure going up again.

There was something clinging to the other side of the door,
but Manning ignored it for the moment. He leaned against the
wall of the room and gratefully sucked air into his lungs. Across
the room, Xelia Zon was doing the same, his nose slowly turning
to its normal color.

"That was a close one," Manning said, finally straightening
up. "A little more and I might not have been able to reach the
door."

Xelia Zon's gaze was riveted on the door. "What's that?" he
asked pointing.

The thing on the door looked like a huge balloon covered
with short fur. It was perfectly round, perhaps two feet in diameter, and at first glance seemed to have no appendages.

Manning looked at it with interest. "I never saw one before,"
he said, "but I suddenly remember hearing about it on the
encyclotape. Come over here and look at it."

Xelia Zon joined him as he bent over to look at it. On closer
examination, they could see that there was a small mouth which
was glued to the keyhole. Even as they watched, the mouth muscles
relaxed and the ball dropped slowly. It bounced on the floor once
and then began floating out into the corridor. Manning reached
out and grabbed it. He held it by the short fur, and the ball slowly
revolved as though the round, pursed mouth were searching.

"What is it?" Xelia asked again.

"An Acruxian pet," Manning said. "It's native to Acrux and every Acruxian has at least one for a pet. Normally, they fill themselves with just enough air to float around. But if they're removed from Acrux, they become ravenous for air.[7] Only they can't suck up enough unless they find some sort of container with a hole about the size of their mouth. I guess these modern, air-tight rooms are perfect for them."

"A pet?" Xelia said. He shivered. "That's not my idea of a pet. It could have killed us."

"I think that was the idea," Manning said. He bounced the *Heliumitis* on the floor like a basketball and caught it. "This, however, is about the only circumstance under which it would try to kill us, so we shouldn't blame it too much."

"Dtilla or Velmar Shonda?"

"Maybe both. No—it couldn't have been Velmar. The door was open when she left and remained open until you arrived. Besides," he added dryly, "she couldn't have been carrying it. She had no place of concealment this large. It must have been Dtilla or one of his friends. Probably hid on this floor, maybe in another room, and waited until we were in here. And that's probably the explanation of Chaun Cla. He was giving somebody the chance to sneak up here in advance."

"What about that thing?" asked Xelia, indicating the ball. "Hadn't we better turn it over to Central Security?"

---

7   The *Heliumitis Acruxa* is a small animal indigenous to the planets in the system of Acrux. It is a very simple organism, deriving all of its nourishment from air. Normally it keeps itself inflated to about a foot in diameter, constantly drawing in enough air to feed itself and to maintain that size. But if it is removed from Acrux, it immediately becomes obsessed with the desire to return and spends all of its time trying to obtain enough air to increase its size to the point where it can escape the gravity of whatever planet it is on. One *Heliumitis* has been known to create a complete vacuum in a spaceship within a period of three hours and the destruction of at least one ship and its entire crew is known to have been so caused. In the early days, when Acrux was first discovered, a number of these creatures were taken to Terra. Immediately afterward there was an epidemic of flat tires on surface cars and it was two weeks before it was discovered that the damage was due to the animals. Since that time, their possession has been outlawed on Terra, although in every other respect they are harmless.

"Why?" Manning asked. "It's harmless enough. That mouth is the only surface organ it has and it doesn't consume anything but air. You Regulusians drive surface cars—you must have places where you can put air in your tires."

"Of course, but—"

"That's it, then," Manning said. "We'll take it down and attach it to an air hose. When it's had enough air, it'll float away and we'll never see it again."

"But if Dtilla did this thing, shouldn't he be arrested?"

"On what charge?"

"Attempted murder. You said yourself that he must have done this."

"I'm sure he did," Manning said, "but we wouldn't have a chance of proving it. The most we could prove is that he was careless in letting his pet get away. Since this is the sort of pet every Acruxian has, we couldn't prove that he brought it to Regulus for a sinister purpose. Even though a Federation court would lean on our side, Dtilla could just laugh us off. And it would be a big mistake."

"How?"

"Since we couldn't prove anything, having him arrested would do nothing except give Acrux an excuse for declaring war against the Federation. If we handed Dtilla to the Federation, they'd drop him like a hot rocket."

"But why?" persisted Xelia. "Surely the Federation could win any war with Acrux and her satellites."

"Maybe," Manning said. "But I think the government is afraid that there might not be any Federation. You yourself have spoken about how the Achernarians feel about Regulusians. Well, you can multiply that over and over. Capellans hate the Polluxians, the Procyonese hate the Arcturusians, Vegans hate the Achernarians—and there are groups on Terra who hate everyone except themselves. All of this could make some little clambake.... Well, let's take bouncing-boy here downstairs for his airing."

CHAPTER FIVE

M ANNING DRACO was up early the following morning. After breakfast in his room, he went to the lobby and arranged to hire a car and driver. He knew that Xelia would have taken him anywhere he wanted to go, but he had at least one visit to make which would be more successful if he was alone.

When the rented car arrived, he directed the driver to take him to the Achernarian Embassy.

It was considerably larger than any other building he had seen, extending back from the street almost twice as far as the average Regulusian building,

Having the driver wait, Manning stood in front of a viewing plate and requested an interview with Seero Sna, Ambassador from Achernar. He identified himself as a political observer from the government and tried to imply that he was completely non-partisan. After a moment the door clicked open and a voice invited him to take the elevator to the lowest floor.

In terms of stories, the building was also larger than the average. Manning counted twelve floors before the elevator stopped. As he stepped out, a voice asked him to walk through the house and into the garden.

It was then that he discovered that in one respect the house was smaller than he'd thought. From the street level it had seemed to be twice as long as the ordinary house; actually it was narrow, extending back the length of one room. Beyond that was the garden.

The garden was the biggest surprise of all. For a moment after stepping into it he could have sworn he was on the Achernarian planet. It was filled with the flowering shrubs and trees native to Achernar and the air was heavy with the scent of the blossoms. Above, it extended for the full twelve stories. At the very top there was a transparent container in which there was a small nuclear machine creating subatomic energy. It was an exact duplicate of the Achernarian sun, built to scale so that the heat from it felt the same as if he had been standing under the real thing on Achernar. Although he could not look directly at it, its appearance seemed to be in perfect scale, too. Small artificial clouds floated lazily over the garden.

"Well, what do you want?" an irritable voice asked. This time there was no evidence of amplification so he knew it was coming directly from the Ambassador. He looked around until he located the Achernarian stretched out in a sort of hammock beneath one of the trees.

ACHERNARIANS BELONG to the Hymenoptera order. That is to say that they are bees, in much the same sense that Terrans are primates—but quite different from any bees which Terrans had seen prior to space flight. The average Achernarian—and the Ambassador was considered an average political-type Achernarian[8]—was about two feet from end to end. He could walk upright or in the manner usually expected of insect life, being equipped with four feet, of which the two front feet could serve as an extra pair of hands when he chose to walk upright. What had once been the front feet, that is the third pair, had evolved into a pair of small hands with double thumbs, so that the Achernarians were the cleverest craftsmen in the Federation.

He still had wings, although they were no longer strong enough to support his body. He wore a robe which bore the same gold and brown markings as his body. It was difficult to tell when he was dressed and when he was not.

The advantages which evolution had granted the Achernarians had been accompanied by certain disadvantages. One had been a weakening of their many-faceted eyes, so that the Ambassador, like most of those from his planet, wore glasses. What had been gained in intelligence had been lost in physical strength; in spite of this, they were among the most ferocious of Federation citizens, the Achernarian soldiers wearing atomic-

---

8   It is interesting to note that the type of Achernarian who went in for political life consisted of those who in a more primitive state would have been known as drones.

powered armor which made them almost invincible.

"Hello," Manning Draco said when he finally located the Ambassador. "May your day be filled with blossoms." It was a stock expression of politeness.

"It might be if I weren't interrupted so often," the Ambassador snapped. It was also normal for Achernarians to be irritable; if Seero Sna exceeded the norm it was a result of having been sent to Regulus. "What do you want, Terran?"

"I am here to observe the election," Manning said. "Consequently, I am interested in the fact that an Acruxian is the sole candidate for the Senate from here. I understand that this Dtila Raishelle has called upon you."

"Yes."

"Why did he come to see you?"

"Because he's an idiot," the Ambassador said waspishly.[9] "On his first visit, he wanted to arrange a trade agreement with us. He seemed to be rather proud of a type of blossom grown on his home planet and thought he could sell them to us. He had a sample with him. It was horrible. I told him so. Nobody can match the quality of Achernarian blossoms."

"That's certainly true," Manning said. "What about his second and third visits?"

"Same thing," grumbled the Achernarian. "He kept insisting that we could learn to like their blossoms. I don't know when I've met anyone so dense."

"Why didn't you report his visits to the Federation?"

"Why should I? If I reported every idiot who approaches me, I'd get nothing else done."

"Didn't it occur to you that he might have been trying to get some other information out of you? Perhaps something inimical to the Federation or to Achernar?"

"Nonsense," snapped the Ambassador. "He was very nice.

---

9 It is believed that there was a strain of wasp somewhere in Seero Sna's family line.

He was especially sympathetic to my position on this accursed planet. He'll probably make a very fine senator."

"No doubt," Manning said dryly. "Did you happen to notice if he was carrying some sort of luggage? A rather large box, in fact?"

THE AMBASSADOR thought a moment, crushing a handful of blossoms and waving them near his face. "I believe he was carrying some sort of covered box."

"Covered?"

"Yes."

"You're sure?"

"Of course, I'm sure. I'm always sure. What's so important about a box?" He looked up at Manning with a shrewd expression in his eyes. "You think, perhaps, he's carrying around a ballot box which he'll switch for the official one on election day? If so, I trust you will remember that this is a practice which was started on Terra and, therefore, he could have learned none of the fine points of this art from me."

"I'll remember," Manning said, grinning. "By the way, don't you have any servants?"

"Certainly I have servants. Fifty of them, if you must know."

"Why don't they answer the door and conduct visitors to you?"

"Do you think I would endanger their lives?" demanded the Ambassador. "Do you realize that these Regulusians are barbarians? Why, they've always eaten my kind, and we Achernarians are not fooled by their claim that they've given up this horrible practice. They should never have been admitted to the Federation, and I'm warning you—you may report this to Terra—that my planet is fully prepared to protect its citizens. An act of aggression will not go unanswered."

"Sure," Manning said soothingly. "Say, do you have a visiscreen here?"

"Of course, I do. Do you think I'm a primitive? I'm tired of your questions, Terran. Go away. But don't forget to tell your Regulusian friends what I've said. Not a single act of aggression will go unanswered. Any attack on me, or my staff, will mean war."

"I'll tell them," Manning said. He turned and walked back across the garden.

"Be sure the door locks after you," the Achernarian called after him. "These Regulusian hoodlums would love to find me vulnerable."

Manning nodded and continued on his way without answering. He knew from experience that there was no point in arguing with an Achernarian. Once one of them got an idea, it took more than words to change it.

Out on the street again, he climbed into the car and asked the driver to take him to the spot where he and Xelia had come below the surface on the day before.

Again he had the driver wait and he took the elevator up to the kiosk. A moment later, he was in his ship.

First, he put through a visicall to his office on Terra. After finding out that business was going on as usual, he told his secretary some things he wanted her to send him immediately by carrier jet. He turned on the receiver beam in his ship and then put through a call to J. Barnaby Cruikshank over a tight-beam.

"Well, Manning, my boy," J. Barnaby said when the connection was made. "Everything all settled, eh? I knew you—"

"Everything isn't all settled," Manning interrupted. He quickly sketched in what he had learned, leaving out his guesses. He also left out any mention of Velmar Shonda.

"Then why are you wasting time calling me?" demanded J. Barnaby. "Don't you realize that tomorrow is election day? Get on the ball, boy."

"I want you on it with me," Manning said dryly. "There are a couple of little things I want you to do."

"What?"

"I suppose you want this Acruxian handled with soft gloves?"

"Absolutely," J. Barnaby said. "I don't care what you do to him, you understand, as long as nothing can be proved against us. But it's imperative that the government not be involved."

"Sure," Manning said. "I suppose it would be all right if I went to prison, or something like that, as long as you're in the clear. Some day, J. Barnaby, I'm going to let you stew in the juice you're always cooking up for me…. What if I can have the Acruxian arrested?"

"No," J. Barnaby said explosively. "Unless he's caught red-handed in the commission of a very serious crime, he must not be arrested. It would have to be something so serious that the Acruxian government would have to refuse to recognize him. Any intent will not be enough."

"Okay, then. I want you to send a complete visicast crew here at once. They should be here in time to be set up and ready to make a Federation-wide visicast by eight tonight. Then you'll have to clear the time and see to it there are a number of spot announcements concerning a special visicast. We want as wide an audience as possible, especially on Achernar."

"I guess that can be done. But it better be worth it. There'll be hell to pay if all that preparation is made and nothing comes of it."

"Something will come of it," Manning promised. "Oh, another thing, J. Barnaby. You have any objections to me running for the Senate?"

"What? What kind of a hold-up is this? You know, very well that the party has made air of its nominations long ago. The elections take place tomorrow—"

"Watch your blood pressure," Manning said with a grin. "I meant if I become a candidate for the Senate from Regulus."

"What about Xelia Zon?" J. Barnaby asked.

"He's no longer in the race. This is part of my plan."

J. Barnaby's face was still flushed with suspicion. "All right," he said. "But don't get any ideas—"

"How you talk," Manning said and, cut the connection.

NEXT, HE PUT IN a call to Vega. He had her hold young Barnaby up to the screen and listened in delight to the gurgling sounds which seemed perfectly intelligible to him. Then he told her that he'd probably be home sometime the following day.

"That'll be wonderful, darling," Vega said. "We miss you…. Manning?"

"Mmmm?"

"No girls?"

"No girls," he said, feeling a twinge of guilt about the Aldebaranese.

She blew him a kiss and the connection was broken.

Manning knew that he would have to wait almost two hours before the carrier jet would arrive. He dug through his library and found an encyclotape on Aldebaran. He put it on and turned the switch, adjusting the tape so as to skip the physical description of the system.

"…The people of Aldebaran III are evolved from one of the two thousand known forms of the order of Chiroptera. Unlike those found in other parts of the Federation, however, they have become completely humanoid in the process of evolution. They have retained none of the physical characteristics of their order or genus, although many of their habits are still related to those of their primitive ancestors. It is believed that the Aldebaranese of the third planet are descended from the genus *Phyllostoma-tidae* since they are almost entirely fruit eaters. Judged by human standards, they are quite attractive, the females being especially beautiful. They seem to be sexually attracted to humans and other humanoid races and there are records of a number of mutually satisfactory unions. The Aldebaranese of the fourth planet are quite different in—"

Manning cut off the switch. He had been curious about Velmar Showda, but she came from the third planet and there was no point in listening to the dry, academic description of her cousins on the other planets. He replaced the encyclotape with a music tape and settled back to wait for the carrier jet.

CHAPTER SIX

TWO HOURS later, a light glowed on the instrument panel of the *Alpha Actuary*, indicating that the carrier had come to rest in the receiver-lock. Manning waited a few minutes, then opened the inner door to the lock. He opened the carrier and took the two small packages it contained. One was a completely sealed canister which buzzed when he held it up to his ear. The other was a large bouquet of flowers, fresh-sealed so that they would keep indefinitely.

Putting the two packages in a hand-pack, Manning left the ship and went back to the kiosk. When he reached the underground level, he ordered the driver back to the hotel.

There were two people waiting in the lobby for him. One of them was Velmar Shonda. Her yellow eyes lighted up at the sight of him.

"Manning," she exclaimed, coming to meet him. She put her hand over his and the touch of her fingers was enough to make a man forget his good intentions. "I came to ask you to take me to a party. Afterward, I thought we could drive out in the country. There's a wonderful little place I've found and I'd like to share it with you."

Manning was acutely aware of her nearness, of the warm scent washing over him. He was also aware of Xelia Zon waiting in the background and the memory of a voice saying, "No girls." A small part of him wanted to go with the Aldebaranese, while a greater part of him knew it would be trading larger happiness for a desire of the moment. He shook his head.

"Sorry, honey," he said, feeling as if he'd been saying nothing else. "Xelia Zon is waiting for me."

For a brief minute a new and harder expression crept into her golden eyes. "You're a strange man, Manning," she said—"or a strong one."

"What do you mean?"

"I meant it as a challenge," she said provocatively.

When her meaning penetrated, Manning laughed. "I got news for you, sweetheart," he said, "but it'll have to wait. Run along now."

He watched the provocative swing of her hips as she walked away. Then he turned and joined Xelia Zon.

"You seem to be very popular," Xelia said dryly. "I, too, have been waiting for you. You have been busy?"

"I went up to the ship to call my wife." Manning grinned. "To assure her that I was resisting temptation. Now, I'd like to go talk to the Security officers who have been trailing Dtilla Raishelle."

Xelia Zon's tail twitched questioningly, but he said nothing as he led the way to his car. They drove directly to the Central Security offices, where Manning spent the next hour talking to the two officials who had followed the Acruxian since he landed on the planet. After considerable prodding, they did remember that his box had been covered each time he'd called on the Achernarian ambassador. They couldn't remember having seen it covered at any other time.

WHEN THEY LEFT Central Security, Manning asked Xelia to take him to the nearest Regulusian real estate office. After listening patiently to a long sales talk on the advantages of the better residential sections, Manning bought a house. He gave the agent a certified credit draft and they left.

"How long," he asked Xelia, "will it be before the purchase of the house will be officially registered?"

"Probably within a few minutes. He'll make an official deposit of the transfer as quickly as he can for fear you'll change your mind—since he charged you about twenty percent more than the property is worth. As soon as the deposit is made, the registry is flashed in all realty offices throughout the planet, and you'll be recognized as a resident of Regulus. But why?"

"I want to become a candidate for the Regulusian Senate seat," Manning said. "How do I go about this?"

"Why?" asked the astonished Xelia. "Tomorrow is election

day. Even if you could overcome my people's antipathy to Terrans, there isn't enough time to reach all the voters. You forget that we have no visicasting system."

"I could get enough votes if I were the only candidate."

"You're going to challenge Dtilla Raishelle?"

"Something like that," Manning admitted. "Actually, whether I'm elected or not is only a by-product. How do I become a candidate?"

"Well," Xelia said, "there are several ways. Let's see...." He raised one hand to glance at the finger-time. "One method is to have a supporter declare your intention at any organized political meeting. There is one being held very shortly at the home of Brono Pia."

"Do you think Dtilla Raishelle will be there?"

"Probably. Brono Pia is one of his supporters. But—but, Manning, you can't be serious about this. You must know that no Terran has a chance against an Acruxian. Do you have a plan?"

"Of sorts," Manning said. "I think I know what is in Dtilla's precious box and it isn't perfume, even though it smells. And I think I know his plan."

"What?"

"It's simply a matter of knowing the value of *p* to the *k* power," Manning said, grinning.[10] Obviously he was not going to say any more. "Now, let's go to the party. Will you be my supporter and declare my intentions?"

"All right," Xelia said glumly, turning his car around.

---

10   Manning Draco had arrived at his conclusions by applying the well-known Pascal and Fermat equation concerning probabilities. This, you will remember, runs:

$$p^k = \frac{n!}{(n-k)!\,k!}\ p^k\,q^{n-k}$$

For ordinary purposes, this equation is quite easy to use, but it is another matter to use it to discover the contents of a mysterious box and the purpose for which it is intended. Figuring *n!* [not to mention *(n-k)* and *k!*] is quite a chore even for Manning Draco.

To Manning's unpracticed eye, the house to which they went looked exactly like the one they had gone to the day before. Again they were met by a butler who escorted them to an elevator and when they reached the lower floor they were met by another servant who led them to a garden with piped-in sunlight. There seemed to be the same crowd there, clustered in little groups. He caught a glimpse of Velmar Shonda, who interrupted her conversation to stare at him with her searching golden eyes, and at one end there was Dtilla Raishelle, surrounded by admiring Regulusians.

The Acruxian caught sight of them as they entered the garden and waved a tentacle in their direction. There was nothing in his manner to indicate that he had made an attempt to eliminate Manning and had failed.

"He seems to have taken last night's failure calmly," Xelia said, keeping his voice down. "You know, I was sure that he'd try again before this."

MANNING SHOOK his head. "According to the encyclotape, Acruxian psychology doesn't work that way. They've very apt to make some clever attempt at assassination over the slightest suspicion that you're an enemy, but if that fails—and it doesn't very often—they believe it constitutes a judgment from their gods and then they sit back and wait for you to make the next move. When you do, they're usually more than ready and they seldom fail on the second try—which then proves that the gods have changed their mind. So Dtilla is waiting to see what I intend to do. If you'll go make the announcement, I'll stroll over and try to oblige him."

Leaving Xelia, Manning strolled across the garden, being sure to give wide berth to Velmar. He moved leisurely, trying to time his movements according to Xelia's progress.

"May your day be fulfilled," the Acruxian called out as Manning drew near.

"And yours," Manning returned politely. Glancing around, he saw Xelia and another Regulusian, who was obviously the host, going to a small stand in the garden. Manning thrust his way through the group that stood around Dtilla Raishelle. As he offered his hand, he glanced down and made sure that the same box reposed on the ground beside the Acruxian.

Dtilla reached out and coiled a tentacle about Manning's hand. "It is a pleasure to meet a political observer so astute," he said. There was no doubt that he was referring to the night before. If there could have been any doubt, he soon removed it. "I shall miss my little pet, but the gods have truly noted your greatness."

"Thanks," Manning said. Then, still holding Dtilla's tentacle, he kicked as hard as he could against the side of the box on the ground.[11]

Manning couldn't be certain, but it seemed to him that the box almost tipped over and that the tipping started even before his foot reached it. He also thought that the top of the box started to rise just before two of the Acruxian's tentacles clamped down on it. But whether he was right or not wasn't important; the reaction of Dtilla Raishelle was.

"*Dtona grooush!*" he shouted angrily. No one there could understand the shout, since it was not in Acruxian but in some obscure dialect, but it was obviously either a curse or a command. At the same moment, the tentacle which still held Manning's hand tightened in an almost bone-crushing grip. There was an expression of murderous anger in the eye-stalks as they inclined toward Manning.

"You—" he began.

"Your attention, please," another voice called out, interrupting the Acruxian. It was the Regulusian host and he seemed amused. "Our good friend, Xelia Zon, wishes to make a declaration of political importance. You will kindly give him your attention." He stepped down from the small stand and Xelia Zon took his place.

---

11   On Acrux, the supreme insult that can be offered an individual is to strike or in any way attack his personal property, since Acruxians consider material possessions immeasurably superior to the person.

"My friends," said Xelia, "I have come before you this afternoon to place in nomination for the office of Regulusian Senator to the Assembly of Stars of the Federation the name of that stalwart son of Terra, that friend of the people, that intrepid defender of Regulusian rights—Manning Draco!"

"Hear, hear!" a number of Regulusians murmured politely.

"So," exclaimed Dtilla Raishelle, once more bending his angry eye-stalks toward Manning, "not only have you insulted me in a more despicable fashion than I have ever been insulted before, but you also dare to oppose my election. It will give me great pleasure to challenge you to a duel which must be held before the, election. You are challenged to meet me tonight in the central Arena."

"I accept," said Manning, disentangling his hand from the tentacle which still grasped it. "As the challenged party, I believe I have the right to name the method by which the duel will be fought."

"That is correct," the Acruxian said. He waved his tentacles angrily. "But understand, Terran, in regard to the political aspects of our duel, almost any of the legal tests of Regulus will do, but since a personal insult is also involved I warn you that the duel must be such as to satisfy my honor."

"I'll satisfy your honor," Manning said dryly. "I suggest a duel by tri-blast." He indicated the three-barreled weapon in the holster attached to the Acruxian's skirt as the surrounding Regulusians gasped. "I trust you have a spare weapon with you so that I may be accommodated in the duel?"

"I have a spare tri-blast," Dtilla said. There was speculation mixed with the anger in his eyes.

"I trust this will satisfy your honor," Manning said formally.

"As you must know, the tri-blast is the best method of satisfying honor," Dtilla said. "Are you familiar with the weapon?"

"No, but I imagine I can become so. Sufficiently for the purpose. Shall we say at eight o'clock tonight?"

THE ACRUXIAN nodded. Both the speculation and the anger had melted before the pleasure of his anticipation. It was evident in his eye-stalks and the slight trembling of his tentacles. "That will be fine," he said. "You understand that should you survive, defeat still forces you to withdraw as a candidate?"

"Oh, I understand it," Manning said cheerfully. "Do you?" Without waiting for an answer, he turned on his heel and marched toward the house. Xelia joined him when he was about halfway across the garden. Out of the corner of his eye, Manning saw Velmar Shonda leave the group she was with.

"Can you walk a little faster?" he said to Xelia in an undertone. "I don't feel up to facing that wench just now."

They reached the elevator ahead of her and as the door closed Manning saw that she was giving up the chase.

"Do you really intend to go through with this?" Xelia asked as they reached the street.

Manning nodded. "I was pretty sure earlier that I knew what Dtilla was up to," he said. "Now, I'm positive. I think this is about the only way to stop him safely."

"But do you know what you're getting into?" persisted Xelia. "If those blade guns can amputate all three legs of an Acruxian at one shot, you can imagine what it will do to you. You don't even know how to use the weapon!"

"No, but I can learn tonight."

"Do you really think," Xelia asked in amazement, "that you can kill him or cripple him first?"

"I don't think anyone will be killed or crippled," Manning said lightly. "As near as I can understand, Acruxian honor is a very tricky affair, but there is one out. I'm going to time it to give Dtilla a chance to take that out and I think under the circumstances, he will. Now, I want you to do a couple more things for me, if you will, Xelia."

"Of course. What?"

"There's a visicast crew on its way here. They'll probably land in the next hour or so. Will you meet them and help them to make any necessary arrangements so that the duel between Dtilla and myself can be visicast? Is there any way we can make sure of having a large crowd there tonight?"

"There are always large crowds at challenges. It'll be especially large tonight because of the nature of the duel. You can be sure that everyone will know about it."

"Good. Now, one more thing. Get in touch with your friend at Central Security and have him call off the two officers who have been trailing Dtilla."

"Why?"

"I'm sure Dtilla knows about them and I want him to feel particularly free tonight. Will you do it?"

"If you say so, Manning," Xelia said doubtfully. He looked as if he wasn't sure that Manning hadn't blown a jet.

"No, I haven't gone crazy," Manning said, grinning. "You see, you Regulusians aren't the only ones who can read expressions. Now, run along. You can pick me up at the hotel in time for the duel."

"What are you going to do?" Xelia asked.

Manning grinned again. "I'm going to double-lock my door against visiting Aldebaranese females and get some rest."

CHAPTER SEVEN

IT WAS a little before seven-thirty when Xelia Zon picked up Manning Draco. He assured him that the visicast crew was all set up in the Arena and everything was ready. They climbed into Xelia's car and drove to the Arena.

It was a huge place with a seating capacity of several hundred thousand. Each seat in the Regulusian Arena was equipped with a viewer and a built-in receiver so that each individual could see and hear as if he were within a few feet of the contestants.

It was already packed with Regulusians when Manning arrived. The center of the Arena, perhaps four or five hundred yards in diameter, was brilliantly lighted with the portable floods brought in by the visicast crew, and the cameras were already focused and waiting for the signal from the emergency booth established in the first tier of seats.

Dtilla Raishelle, still carrying his large box, was already there, his green skirt bearing the ceremonial feathers worn by every Acruxian when dueling. He was not exactly pleased to learn that the duel was to be visicast over the Federation network, but there was nothing in the dueling code to prevent this and he accepted it with ill grace. He carried his pair of tri-blasts in a handsome case and according to tradition offered Manning first choice. Manning carelessly took one of them and examined it until he was sure that he knew how it operated. Then he thrust it in his belt.

Taking the remaining blade gun, Dtilla Raishelle picked up his box and moved stolidly into the center of the Arena. Manning Draco waited until he caught a nod from the man in the emergency booth, then he picked up his small hand-pack and walked to the center of the Arena, stopping a few yards away from Dtilla. He knew that the visicast had already started and that an announcer in the booth was explaining the scene to the billions of viewers.

As soon as Manning reached the center of the space, Dtilla Raishelle placed his box on the ground. He lifted the tri-blast and saluted Manning, then began a complicated dance, his tentacles weaving. It was a performance dedicated to the Acruxian gods that preceded every Acruxian duel to death. Manning had heard it described on the encyclotape, but it was fascinating to see it. He knew it would last about three minutes and that no Acruxian could honorably kill or maim until the dance was finished. Once it was completed, however, there was no way an Acruxian could withdraw from a duel; until it was over there were a number of proscribed emergencies which would permit him to honorably quit the field.

Manning knew he had no more than about two and a half minutes in which to act—and he'd really be out of luck if his guess was wrong. Manning began a peculiar dancing motion of his own and suppressed a grin as he caught sight of the announcer's face in the emergency booth. Manning was doing a rough imitation of an ancient Terran tribal dance he had once seen on an ancestor-film. He knew that the announcer had been gaily explaining the ceremonial dance of the Acruxian, but was being completely baffled by the prancing of his fellow Terran.

He saw Dtilla glance curiously at him once, but that was all from him. Manning had gambled on the chance that the Acruxian had never before dueled a Terran and so would be willing to believe that they too had ceremonial dances.

As he danced around, drawing ever nearer to the box on the ground, Manning Draco unfastened the opening of his hand-pack and took from it the fresh-sealed flowers. He broke the seal and began to strew the flowers around. Seemingly by accident, when he'd finished, the flowers formed a circle around the box that belonged to the Acruxian.

Manning removed the second package, broke the seal, and threw it on the ground near the flowers. As it struck the ground, the canister split into two sections.

At that moment, Manning motioned to those in the booth and a super-spot was thrown on the circle of flowers as one of the overhead cameras swung in for a close-up. It was just in time to catch the sight of a number of tiny objects rising swiftly from the two halves of the canister. They hovered there a moment, then spread out and approached the flowers. The microphones picked up the steady buzzing sound.

Manning Draco cast aside the hand-pack as he moved backward. Then he drew the tri-blast and waited.

ALTHOUGH NO ONE in the Arena, or among the billions viewing it at home, knew what was happening, a tense hush fell over them. There was such an air of suspense that the Acruxian felt it and faltered in his dance.

So slowly that at first no one believed it was happening, the top half of the big box in the center of the flowers began swinging upward. The first one who was sure of what he saw was the Acruxian.

"Dtona grooush!" he shouted. He shouted something else in

the same tongue; he had started to run toward the box, then halted as he realized that his dance had carried him too far away.

The top of the box continued to rise, slowly as though someone, or something, didn't want to attract attention.

Then the top was all the way up and there was a wind-like sound as thousands of Regulusians released their pent-up breath. Many light-years away, other viewers tensed in front of their visiscreens.

What came out of the box was undoubtedly a bird, but unlike one ever seen in the Federation. From head to tail it was a good three feet long and, standing, it was about two feet tall. Its feathers were brown and white, with a black stripe running across its eyes like a mask. What had once been wings were now wing-like arms ending in a pair of three-fingered hands. There was an intelligent cruelty in its yellow eyes. A strange-

looking harness was strapped around its body and in it there was a needle-sharp weapon.

As the bird came out of the box, it had eyes only for the small objects which buzzed around the flowers. Its head shot out again and again and each time its beak closed on one of the buzzing objects.

Manning Draco shouted and the bird glanced up. It looked at the man who stood before it and its beak yawned widely. There was a brief glimpse of a double row of teeth. Then it moved toward him, its eyes bright with intent. One hand crept toward the weapon in its harness.

Manning Draco fired the tri-blast. There was a sharp energy recoil and then the three blades struck the bird. It cried out something in the strange dialect the Acruxian had used and tried to dodge at the last moment, but it was too late. Feathers swirled in the air and then it went down, neatly sliced into four parts.

The cameras followed Manning Draco as he walked over to the dead bird and they moved in for a close-up. Off to one side, Dtilla Raishelle, reduced from co-star to extra, was ignored.

Manning scooped up one of the small objects, wincing slightly as it stung him. Then he held up the brown and gold bumblebee so that it could be seen.

"Citizens of the Federation," he said, "the creature which I just killed in self-defense was a Denebian, probably evolved from something very similar to the Terran Shrike, or Butcher Bird. Although the dominant form in their system, the Denebians are a completely ruthless life form, especially destructive toward all form of insects. This Denebian was brought to Regulus by an Acruxian agent and kept concealed in that box. During the past few days, the Denebian was permitted no food. It was planned to turn the Denebian loose in the Achernarian Embassy here, believing that inevitably the killing of the Achernarians would be blamed on the Regulusians and cause civil war in the Federation. This—"

Suddenly there was an interruption which Manning Draco had not planned. Velmar Shonda came running out into the Arena and threw her arms around Manning.

"MY HERO," she exclaimed. Her mouth pressed hotly against his.

Up in the emergency booth, the announcer quickly began an excited commentary on what they had just seen, while the cameras swung around to focus on the Acruxian. But he was no longer in the Arena.

In the meantime, with the aid of a couple of attendants, Manning succeeded in prying the Aldebaranese away from him. His mouth stung, and wiping his hand across it, he discovered it was bleeding. Velmar Shonda had bitten his lip.

The announcer in his booth finished his comments and the visicast was switched back to the home studios where another announcer was ready to more clearly tie this incident in with the galactic situation.

"Visicast over," the director shouted over the Arena audio system.

At that moment, a Vegan, in the uniform of the Federation Patrol, came running onto the field. As he neared them, there was a shrill scream from Velmar Shonda. She broke away from the attendants and started to run, but she didn't get far.

The Vegan patrolman drew a large-barreled gun from his holster and fired. Velmar Shonda thrashed around inside a force-net that held her prisoner.

"Boy," exclaimed the young patrolman, "am I glad I saw that!"

"Saw what?" Manning asked.

"I was on patrol just above this planet," the Vegan explained, "and I was watching the visicast from here when she ran out and attacked you. I blasted down and got here as fast as I could, but I don't mind admitting I was scared she'd get away."

"Attacked me?" Manning said. "I'm afraid you've made a mistake, officer. All she did was kiss me."

The Vegan shook his head. "Your lip is bleeding, isn't it?" Manning nodded and the patrolman went on: "It was an attack, sir. I know this one. She's Velmar Shonda from Aldebaran IV. We've been looking for her for two months."

Manning was dazed. "Did you say Aldebaran IV? She said she was from the third planet."

"She's from the fourth one, sir. Oh, they look a lot like the Aldebaranese on III—except for the golden eyes. You can always tell them by that."

"But—but," stammered Manning, remembering, "the ency-clotape said that the inhabitants on the fourth planet are very different…"

"They are—in their habits," the patrolman said grimly. "This baby eats nothing but blood and she could drain you in about an hour."[12]

"If that's true," Xelia Zon said excitedly, "then that must account for the Regulusians who have been vanishing."

"If any of you have been vanishing," the patrolman said, "then this baby is probably the reason for it. She's got a big appetite. Boy, am I glad I found her. Well—"

Another Regulusian came rushing up. "The Acruxian," he exclaimed. "He's escaped!"

"He can't get far," Xelia said grimly. "He didn't have a ship here. Unless he steals your ship, Manning."

"If he tried that, he'd be in for a surprise," Manning said.

"An Acruxian?" the patrolman asked. "I saw one on the surface

---

12   As Manning would have learned if he hadn't been so impatient to turn off the encyclotape, the inhabitants of Aldebaran IV, while also belonging to the order of Chiroptera, are evolved from the genus Desmodus rotundus, vulgarly known on Terra as the Vampire Bat. They are exclusively blood eaters, preferring the blood of primates and in modern times having a special preference for the blood of humans. For this reason, their planet had been in strict quarantine, but Velmar Shonda had somehow escaped and hid out on Regulus. Having main-tained the feeding habits of their primitive ancestors while they had physically evolved along humanoid lines, it was little wonder that the females like Velmar were known as Vampires in every sense of the word.

as I came in. There was another ship coming in from one of the satellites of Regulus. Come to think of it, it looked as if it might be under remote control."

"I thought he'd have a ship hidden somewhere," Manning said. "He's gone, then." He sounded cheerful.

"You want this Acruxian for something?" the patrolman asked.

"No," Manning said quickly before anyone else could answer.

"Okay. I'll be getting in with my prisoner. She ought to get me a promotion. And thanks, chum, for letting her bite your lip, so I could see her."

"Think nothing of it," Manning said, rubbing his lip, as the patrolman went away, dragging Velmar still in the force-net.

When it was all over, Manning realized that he was tired. He didn't feel like the trip back to Terra, so he went to the hotel and went to bed. He slept the sleep of the just and by the time he awakened the following morning, he was the duly elected Senator of Regulus. There was quite an official party to see him off.

CHAPTER EIGHT

I T WAS MIDDAY when Manning Draco landed back on Terra. He took an aircab to his pent-estate and went eagerly into the house. He wondered why Vega hadn't come to meet him, but then he thought she hadn't heard the cab arrive.

She was in the sun room. Manning bounded into the room and threw out his arms. "Hi, honey," he said.

She didn't answer.

"Hey," he said. "What's the matter? I'm home. Is there something wrong with Barnaby, or what?"

Vega finally consented to look up. "My hero!" she said scornfully.

Ouch! He'd forgotten that Velmar's capture hadn't been visicast; he'd even forgotten that Vega might have been watching the cast.

"Wait a minute," he said indignantly. "You got me all wrong. I couldn't stop her from running out and kissing me like that when I didn't even know she was coming. Besides, she wasn't kissing me—she was biting me."

"A big difference!"

"You bet it was. A Federal Patrolman arrived right afterwards to arrest her. She'd escaped from Aldebaran IV. Hey, don't you understand? She was a vampire from that quarantined planet. All she was out for was blood—not me."

"So you invited her up to your room to see your veins," Vega said. "Etchings—veins—what's the difference?"

"I got witnesses," Manning said desperately.

"I'll say you have," Vega said bitterly. "Billions of them. Do you know how many women called up to see if I'd been watching the visicast? And to think that I had to be holding little Barnaby up to look at the screen at that very moment."

"Look, honey, that dame—hell, you couldn't even call her a dame—was really dangerous. She was helping Dtilla Raishelle, but on the side she'd already helped herself to ten Regulusians. I was next on the list—"

Just then the door-announcer chimed. Before either of them could go to answer it, they heard the door open.

"Anybody home?" a voice called. It was J. Barnaby Cruikshank.

"Come in here," Manning yelled.

J. Barnaby appeared a moment later, his face beaming and his clothes looking so well-groomed he was hardly recognizable. "Manning, my boy," he said expansively, "you did it."

"I'll say he did," muttered Vega.

"You were magnificent," J. Barnaby continued before Manning could say anything. "I've read all the reports and you were never better. The way you reasoned that Dtilla Raishelle visited the Achernarian Ambassador three times in order to familiarize himself with the lock so he'd have no trouble picking it when he returned to toss that Denebian inside—it was superb."

"J. Barnaby—" began Manning.

"And," interrupted J. Barnaby, "I will never know how you managed to figure out that the Acruxian was carrying a Denebian in that box, or how you knew the Denebian could see through the box. It was superlative!"

"Oh, it wasn't much," said Manning, caught off-guard for the moment. "I knew that the Acruxians had used Denebians before and the fact that Dtilla covered the box when he went to the Achernarian Embassy made it easy to guess the box was made with one-way-vision plastic. After that, it was only a matter of learning the value of *(n-k)!* and—to hell with *(n-k)!!* J. Barnaby, you've got to—"

"My boy," interrupted J. Barnaby, "we owe you more than we can ever pay you. Not only did you handle the matter so that the Acruxians can't make any complaint, since Dtilla escaped, but the Achernarians were so impressed by the visicast that most of them voted for our party instead of their own. It was a Republocrat victory by a landslide."

"That's nice," Manning said hurriedly. "Now, will you tell—"

"I knew the minute I heard of the problem," J. Barnaby said expansively, "that Manning Draco was the boy who would soon have the situation well in hand."

"He had it well in hand, all right," Vega said.

"J. Barnaby," Manning said desperately, "you've got to tell Vega about that Aldebaranese. She refuses to believe me and—"

"All I know," J. Barnaby said blandly, "is what I see on the visiscreen."

"Ha!" said Vega.

MANNING DRACO stared at his father-in-law in amazement. Then anger took over. "So," he said, "you owe me more than you can ever pay me, do you, you old double-crossing Spican termite. I've put up with a lot from you, J. Barnaby Cruikshank, but I'll get you for this where it hurts if it's the last thing I do. I'm a member of the Senate now and when I take office I'm going to start a campaign to get a new Secretary of Planets."

"That's what I dropped in about," J. Barnaby said. "It seems that you are no longer a senator."

"What?"

"My boy," J. Barnaby said paternally, "while you were on Regulus, you should have paid more attention to the—er—sexual habits of the Regulusians."

"What's that got to do with it?"

"Everything. Regulusians consider sex as a very serious game, sort of a battle of the sexes as it were, just as they do everything else. It is not a separate part of their lives. Therefore, a sexual challenge is judged just the same as any other challenge. It is known all over Regulus that this Aldebaranese—Velmar Shonda, or some such name—constantly challenged you in a sexual way and that you just as constantly refused to accept the challenge. Why, you even blatantly shoved her away from you in the Arena—calling on two attendants to help you in this unmasculine action—in full view of several hundred thousand Regulusians."

"What of it?" Manning demanded harshly.

"Unfortunately, my boy, as a result of refusing a challenge—you may recall the laws about a political candidate refusing challenges—your election was questioned. The Regulusian Lower Court—the highest in the land, by the way—ruled against you. They couldn't have done otherwise, considering the evidence. Luckily, by the use of a little influence, we were able to have a good Republocrat, Xelia Zon, appointed to finish your term."

But neither Manning nor Vega heard his last sentence. They had turned to look at each other as they realized the meaning of what he was saying.

"Oh, darling," said Vega as she came into his arms, "I'm so sorry. How could I have ever doubted you?"

For once, Manning was smart. He didn't even try to answer that question. Instead, he bent his head and kissed her.

When they came up for air, several minutes later, neither of them spoke. They stared deeply into each other's eyes, then, moved by a common thought, they turned and walked in the direction of their bedroom.

They didn't even hear J. Barnaby Cruikshank chortling happily as he let himself out of the house.

ACT TWO / FALL 3473

MISSION TO MIZAR

CHAPTER ONE

IT'S A BUSY universe, and Rigil Kentaurus was undoubtedly the busiest system of all. The two planets had been taken over by the government in the very beginning of the Federation, partly because of the nearness to Terra ("Only 4.3 light-years on your spaceometer") and partly because both planets were pleasantly habitable for Terrans, and the native Kentaurusian population was small enough to make it an easy task to move them away. The Founding Fathers of the Federation had planned well, making Rigil Kentaurus the only completely self-sufficient system in the galaxy. The second planet was given over to supplying the needs of both planets. It was a masterpiece of industrial ingenuity. Through the control of environment, they were able to raise the foods of every world, so that the government workers of the first planet might have their home products. In addition it was the source of the necessities and luxuries of every planet in the Federation. Due to the second planet, it could be truly said that the galactic representatives on the first planet enjoyed a home away from home.

The elaborate defense installations of Rigil Kentaurus were also on the second planet. It was said that not even a pebble could float within two hundred miles of the two planets without being spotted, tracked down, and destroyed within a matter of seconds. Incoming ships had to identify themselves to the outer patrol ring, five hundred miles from the planets. Many had tried but none had succeeded in passing the outer patrol ring unless they were on legitimate errands and were expected.

The first planet in Rigil Kentaurus was the seat of the Federation government. There were gathered the best brains[13] of 107 planets (or so it was claimed), busily engaged in the affairs of government. The entire planet was covered with buildings—government office buildings, private homes and apartment houses, and a shopping center with several hotels for the benefit of those who had to visit Rigil Kentaurus. The only open spaces were the beautifully landscaped parks.

Manning Draco had landed his ship, the *Alpha Actuary,* on the government port early in the afternoon. Since he had been expected there had been no trouble coming through the patrols and when he landed there was an official air-cab at the port waiting to whisk him across the planet to the offices of the Secretary of Expanding Frontiers. It was a command appearance before the Cabinet member.

After waiting an hour in the anteroom, Manning was finally shown into the presence of the Honorable Patrick Masuko. The Secretary was a middle-aged Terran, obviously aware of the honor bestowed on anyone who was summoned to meet him.

"I'm a very busy man," he said, "but my distinguished colleague, the Secretary of Planets, who I understand is your father-in-law, has suggested that I take the time to learn about your vacation service."

"Fine," Manning said. He launched into a sales talk on the advantages of vacationing on sunny Caph II where, thanks to a Time Fracture, one could spend ten months, yet be gone only two weeks. As he talked, he set up a portable projector and flashed pictures of Caph on the wall. The full-color shots of the blue sand and the towering purple trees were impressive. There were several shots of the massive Draco Hotel where, as Manning

---

13 Saramandi Smith, a political philosopher of the 33rd century, claimed that the political failures of mankind are due to the fact that the best brains are always located in the seat of the government. "Swivel-Chair Thinking," he called it.

pointed out, every luxury and entertainment was provided for guests. "It is especially ideal," he concluded, "for such a busy man as yourself. May I inquire if you were thinking of Caph for your annual vacation?"

"No," said the Secretary. "As a matter of fact, I'm about to marry again—Miss Mathilda Yat-Sen, of the Pan-Galactic Yat-Sens, you know—and I was thinking of my honeymoon."

"Spendid," Manning said. "We consider Caph particularly fine for honeymooners. We have a number of excellent honeymoon cottages, some of them in isolated spots, others near to the games and sense-resorts. I might point out, Mr. Secretary, that a honeymoon on Caph has many advantages. Not only does it prolong the many delights of this special occasion, but if it is so desired—since a two-week honeymoon will mean ten months on Caph—the bride may have her first child before returning. In the case of lower-income families, where the bride works, this enables her to have a child at once without losing more than two weeks from her work. In your own case it would mean that your wife can immediately resume her social obligations without the troublesome problem of trying to conceal a delicate condition."

"Er—yes," mumbled the Secretary. "I will get in touch with you, Mr. Draco."

MANNING TOOK the hint and began to fold up his equipment. "And don't forget, sir, that we provide transportation in the most luxurious space liners. We'll be glad to serve you, Mr. Secretary."

"Naturally," the Secretary said in a matter-of-fact voice. "I was glad to see you, young man. We think very highly of Secretary Cruikshank. He is the highest type of public-spirited citizen."

"I'm sure he is," Manning said and his tongue was only partly in his cheek. At the moment his own opinion of J. Barnaby Cruikshank, the owner of the Greatest Solarian Insurance Company and Manning's former boss, was at its highest. The patronage of high government officials would mean a lot to the Draco Vacation Service and for once it looked as if J. Barnaby was trying to do him a favor.

He left the Expanding Frontiers building and went straight back to the government port. He was filled with kindly thoughts of his father-in-law and had decided he'd have Vega invite him down to Terra for dinner soon.

Manning's ship was surrounded, by men in the familiar yellow uniforms of the Federation Patrol. An officer stepped forward to meet him as he hurried toward it.

"Terran Manning Draco?" he inquired crisply.

"Yes," Manning said. "What's wrong?"

"Nothing serious," the officer said, although his manner indicated that he wasn't certain of this. "The clearance of your ship has been temporarily canceled. The Analyzers have returned an unsatisfactory report and I'm afraid we'll have to hold the ship until we have checked further."

"But that's silly," Manning protested. "I came here at the request of Secretary Masuko, and the Analyzers cleared me on the way in. Nothing can have changed about the ship while I was here, unless you changed it yourself."

"That may well be," the officer said smoothly, "but the ship cannot be cleared to leave Rigil Kentaurus."

Bureaucratic red-tape is annoying under the best of circumstances; it is doubly so when a man is anxious to get home to his wife and child. "How long will it take?" Manning asked curtly.

"It is difficult to say, sir. Not before sometime tomorrow morning."

Manning cursed under his breath. "Where can I rent a ship to take me to Terra?"

The officer shook his head. "I'm sorry, sir, but until your ship is cleared it will be impossible for you to leave. I believe you will find the Terra Hotel very comfortable, sir."

Manning turned and stalked into the terminal. He went into

a visibooth and put in a call to his father-in-law. After patiently identifying himself to at least a dozen undersecretaries, he finally found himself facing J. Barnaby Cruikshank. As usual, J. Barnaby looked as if he were personally saving the universe from disaster, but he recovered enough to express pleasant surprise at hearing from his son-in-law.

Manning thanked J. Barnaby for the interview with the Secretary of Expanding Frontiers, answered questions about Vega and little Barnaby, and finally got around to the matter that was most pressing. He explained the situation which faced him at the government port.

"That's too bad," J. Barnaby clucked sympathetically, "but I'm afraid I can't help you, Manning, my boy. Security is the one branch of government which is barred to the rest of us."

"But it's so damned silly," Manning said. "I was cleared on the way in only three hours ago. It's impossible that there could be some element in my ship that wasn't in it then. The Analyzer must have flipped its lid."

"Very possibly, my boy," J. Barnaby said, "but I'm afraid there's nothing we can do about it. Even the President has to accept the orders of Security. I'll tell you what; you run along and call Vega—she'll understand—and get checked in at the hotel. I'll pick you up later and we'll have dinner together."

"All right," Manning said reluctantly. He broke the connection and went out on the landing patio of the terminal. An aircab took him to the Terra Hotel.

BY THE TIME he had talked to Vega, made gurgling sounds at his son when she held him up in front of the visiphone, and had a shower, he was in much better humor. When J. Barnaby Cruikshank arrived to take him to dinner, he was almost glad to see his father-in-law.

Still in his early forties, J. Barnaby was one of the most successful men in the Federation. He had inherited the insurance company, but it was J. Barnaby himself who had built it into one of the largest and richest monopolies in the galaxy. For several years, Manning Draco had been chief investigator for the Greater Solarian Insurance Company, Monopolated, during which time he and J. Barnaby fought almost continually. Then, at about the same time that Manning married Vega Cruikshank and left to start his own business, J. Barnaby had been invited to become Secretary of Planets in the Federation Cabinet, thus fulfilling a lifelong ambition. For a while after that, amicable relations had existed between the two men. This new friendliness had received a sharp setback when J. Barnaby had forced Manning to do an investigation job for the government, but now that he was apparently trying to help Manning all was once more sweetness and light.

They had dinner in the Senate Restaurant, one of the finest dining spots in the universe. It was a good dinner. For the first time, J. Barnaby seemed to show a genuine interest in Manning's business and as the dinner progressed Manning relaxed.

As they were being served coffee and brandy, the conversation finally swung around to J. Barnaby and his new career.

"Not too good," J. Barnaby said in response to a question as to how it was going. "You know, my boy, there are problems in this job that make running an insurance company seem like a snap. But then you don't want to be bored with my problems...."

"Let's hear them," Manning said. He was in a kindly mood and knew that J. Barnaby wanted to talk.

"As a matter of fact, I have a rather delicate problem on my hands right now. Do you know the system of Mizar?"

Manning shook his head. "I seem to remember that it's a double sun, but that's about all."

"Mizar," said J. Barnaby, "is about to be admitted to the Federation. Officially, the act is to take place in about a month. The only inhabited planet is the first one in the system. There will be some fairly valuable mineral rights on the other planets, although it is not believed there will be any profitable trade with the first planet. The Mizarians are an intelligent people, but industrially they lag behind the rest of us. One factor, however, makes them extremely valuable to us. I might say they are potentially one of the most valuable planets of the Federation."

"Why?"

"The Mizarians," J. Barnaby said, lowering his voice to a confidential tone, "are cryptesthesists."

"Come again," Manning said.

"Cryptesthesists. They are not telepaths in any sense of the word, but they have the ability to know what an opponent's next step will be. In other words, if you were to give them a standard telepathic test with the official Rhine Cards, the Mizarians would be one step ahead of you—they'd know how the cards would fall in the next round."

"And they're not telepaths?"

"No. They can't read minds at all."

"I never heard of such a thing," Manning said.

"This is the first race discovered with this ability." J. Barnaby admitted. "The ancients on Terra believed that certain men had this ability, but they were never able to prove it. We've run every possible test on the Mizarians and there's no doubt they have this ability. Think what an advantage it will be to have our space fleet piloted by Mizarians. Why, they would be unbeatable in battle—if we are ever involved in a war."

"Even against a telepathic race?" Manning asked. He knew that the only strong anti-Federation movement was headed by the Acruxians, who were telepathic.

J. Barnaby nodded. "The Mizarian mind cannot be telepathed and so fighting against a telepathic race wouldn't alter our advantage."

"So what's this about troubles?" Manning asked with a grin. "It sounds to me like good news."

"Except for one thing," J. Barnaby said gloomily. "You know of the situation between the Federation and the Acruxian Axis. So far it has been only a battle of wits, but should the Acruxians get even the slightest advantage, we are convinced that they'd invade the Federation. Right now, the balance of power between us is so delicate that both sides are equally careful. You will recall when you helped us out that it was necessary to permit the Acruxian agent to escape. We didn't dare arrest him. In the same manner, last week they permitted a Federation agent to escape rather than risk an open break with us by arresting him."

"But what does this have to do with Mizar?"

"Recently," J. Barnaby said, "there has been evidence of a growing anti-Federation feeling on Mizar. We have just learned that there are Acruxian agents at work on that planet. Do you remember Dtilla Raishelle?"

Manning nodded. Dtilla Raishelle was the Acruxian agent with whom he had tangled the time J. Barnaby had forced him to go on a government mission.

"Well, we think that Raishelle and possibly two other agents are on Mizar. If this anti-Federation sentiment continues, it's possible that Mizar may yet decide not to join the Federation. In that case, they might then decide to join the Axis of Acrux. If that happens we are certain that we will soon be involved in war."

FOR THE FIRST TIME, Manning's old suspicions of J. Barnaby returned in full force. His father-in-law was telling this story in too complete a manner and his face was wearing a bland expression which Manning knew too well.

"No," he said.

J. Barnaby sighed. "It's true," he admitted, "that I hoped that you might be prevailed upon to go to Mizar and straighten this out. After all, we have very few agents who are capable of standing up against an Acruxian. You are, you must remember, the only Terran who has ever developed a secondary mind shield. There should be certain responsibilities in connection with that."

"No," Manning said again. "It's not as if you didn't have plenty of other agents, even if they're not Terrans, who are capable of doing this job. I will not be browbeaten into pulling more of your chestnuts out of the fire. I'm warning you, J. Barnaby—"

"My boy, you wrong me," J. Barnaby said heartily. "I wouldn't think of tricking you. I'll admit that I was hoping you might volunteer to do this for us, but if you don't care to, then that's all there is to it. I wouldn't think of forcing you into something you don't want to do."

Draco looked at J. Barnaby with mounting suspicion. This was a new Cruikshank, the authenticity of which he seriously doubted. "What are you up to?" he demanded.

"Nothing," J. Barnaby said blandly. "You misunderstand me, my dear boy. If you don't want to go, then we won't talk about it. Let's talk about other things."

To Manning's amazement, they did just that. At first, he was still looking for a trap of some sort—he had never known J. Barnaby to give up on something he wanted—but when the subject still didn't come up, he relaxed. Maybe J. Barnaby really was changing.

Nor did Mizar come up during the rest of the evening. By the time J. Barnaby dropped Manning off at his hotel, the latter was convinced that he'd been unduly suspicious of his father-in-law. He spoke once more with Vega on the visiphone and then went to bed.

HE HAD NO IDEA what time it was when he awoke. For a minute he had no idea what it was that had awakened him. Then, suddenly, he realized that every light in his room was on. He swung his feet to the floor and sat up on the edge of the bed. He looked around the room. Everything seemed to be just as it was when he'd gone to bed, except for the lights. He knew he had turned them off.

On each side of his room there was a door connecting with the adjoining room, so that two or more rooms could be rented as a suite. Suddenly the door on the left opened and a girl ran into the room. Long blond hair streamed back from her head and there was an expression of fright on her face. Even in that momentary glimpse, Manning saw that she was beautiful. She was also quite nude.

Without even seeming to see him, she dashed by, passing so

near to the bed he could have reached out and touched her, and vanished through the door on the other side of the room.

Judging by the expression on her face, Manning expected somebody, or something, to be following her. But no one else came through the door nor was there any further sound. When it was obvious that nothing else was happening, Manning reached over and flipped on the room phone. The screen glowed into life and the face of the night clerk looked out at him.

"Yes, sir?" the clerk asked.

"What the hell's going on in this hotel?" Manning demanded. "I was just awakened by someone's turning on all my lights. Then a beautiful naked girl ran through my room."

"Yes, sir," said the clerk as though this were a common event. He stared at Manning and the light of intelligence dawned on his face. "You wanted her to stop, sir?"

"No," Manning cried. "That is, I would have liked her to stop before she ever got to my room. See that it doesn't happen again."

"Yes, sir," the clerk said again. His face stared out of the screen with interest. "But I must say, sir, that we get very few *complaints* about beautiful nude women being in guests' rooms."

Manning broke the connection angrily. He thought about it a minute and then decided that the girl and the clerk both must have been drunk. He turned the lights off again and went back to sleep.

CHAPTER TWO

MANNING WAS UP early the next morning. The first thing he did was call the government port. He was told politely that his ship still had not been cleared and that he might try them again later. In a vitriolic mood, he ordered his breakfast sent up. He was having his coffee when there was a call for him. It was J. Barnaby.

"How are you this morning, my boy?" he asked. He seemed to be in an unusually good mood.

"Terrible," Manning said sourly.

"Why not drop over to the office after you've finished your breakfast?"

"No," Manning said. "My ship still isn't cleared and I thought I'd go down and try to put a rocket on their tails."

"You come on over here," J. Barnaby said, "and maybe we can do something about it. I just had an idea...."

Manning agreed and the connection was broken. He hurried through his coffee and went downstairs, intending to get an aircab. To his surprise, there was an aircar from the Planet Department waiting for him.

A few minutes later he was being shown into the ornate offices of the Secretary of Planets.

J. Barnaby Cruikshank bounced up cheerfully from behind his desk and shook hands with Manning as if he hadn't seen him in months. There was something else strange about him, but it took Manning several minutes to figure it out. When he did, he didn't understand it. J. Barnaby. who usually looked as if he were sitting in the midst of a ruined world, today gave the appearance of having stopped disaster in its tracks.

"What are you looking so smug about?" Manning asked sourly.

"Smug?" said J. Barnaby. "My dear boy, you misjudge me. I am merely filled with well-being, overwhelmed with a sense of brotherhood, aware of the goodness of life."

"Uh-huh," Manning said dryly. "Well, how about spilling a little of that over in my direction and arranging to have my ship cleared?"

"Just what I was thinking about," J. Barnaby said airily. "I gave the matter much thought last night and this morning, and I think I've hit on it. You remember my remarks last night about Mizar?"

"What does that have to do with it?" Manning asked, suspicions returning in full force.

"Well, if you'd care to take on that little mission for us, I'm sure there would be no problem of getting your ship cleared. After all, it is in the interest of Security to have the Mizarian situation straightened out. It shouldn't take you more than a few days and then you'd be back home."

"So that's the way the jets burn," Manning muttered. "I should have guessed right away that you were back of that in some way. You got me up here by having your friend, the Secretary of Expanding Frontiers, pretend to be interested in Caph, then you had my ship held so I couldn't get away. Well, it won't work. I won't do it."

"You wound me deeply," J. Barnaby said, doing his best to look wounded. "It's just that it occurred to me this would be one way out of your difficulty. As a matter of fact, I'm prepared to go farther. As you know, once Mizar enters the Federation, certain concessions will be open to Federation monopolies. While I can't give you any of the manufacturing concessions, you can have first choice of any of the service concessions."

"You know what you can do with your concessions," Manning said. "The answer is still no. I will not go to Mizar."

J. Barnaby Cruikshank sighed heavily. "I'm sorry you're making it necessary for me to take other steps," he said. He opened a drawer and took out a large photograph, holding it so Manning couldn't see it. "I dislike being put in such a peculiar position by my son-in-law. As much as I sympathize with your—ah—youthful spirits, Vega is my only daughter and I fear that my course is painfully clear."

"What are you talking about?" Manning demanded.

"This," said J. Barnaby, turning the photograph over.

IT WAS A VERY CLEAR picture of a beautiful nude girl running through a hotel room. It had been taken just at the moment she had been passing the bed, on the edge of which Manning Draco was perched. The angle made it look as if he were on the verge of launching a flying tackle after the girl. The fear on the girl's face was quite plain and the expression of open-mouthed surprise on Manning's face might have been taken for one of extreme passion. The implications were hardly subtle.

"I too have had my weak moments," J. Barnaby said, "so I can well understand your—ah—feelings, of the moment. But I very much fear that Vega will fail to understand. Like her mother, she is inclined to have a narrow view of such matters."

Manning gave expression to certain opinions he had long held about J. Barnaby Crnikshank.

"Unfortunately—for you—" the latter continued blandly, "the next room was occupied by a gentleman who possesses a boundless curiosity coupled with a mania for photography."

"Who just happened to be there," Manning added bitterly.

"Precisely," J. Barnaby said. He gazed at the picture with interest. "Quite an attractive lady. As I said, I can hardly blame you—but I fear that my duty to my only child is all too clear...."

"And I suppose," Manning said, "that you might forsake that sacred duty if I agreed to go to Mizar for you?"

J. Barnaby sighed again. "Unfortunately, my duty to my government is an even greater one. As much as my heart bleeds for my little girl, if you were to go to Mizar and be successful, I would have no choice but to destroy this evidence. It wouldn't do to have a hero of the Federation seen in such a light."

"Very pretty," said Manning. "But I still won't do it. Vega will believe me—I can prove that it was not my fault that I had to stay overnight here. I can also prove that I complained to the clerk last night about that woman in my room."

"The clerk," J. Barnaby said mildly, "is under the impression that you were complaining because she didn't stay in your room. As for the rest, there is no record that clearance was refused your ship. Were Vega to decide to check your story—and as her father I would have to advise her to do so—an investigator would learn that there was no reason why you couldn't leave last night. As for the girl, she would have an interesting story to tell if she were forced to testify in court. I fear it would make me look rather bad, even though it is perfectly normal to protect one's son-in-law."

Manning waited, knowing the rest of it would come out.

"Until this morning," J. Barnaby said, "she was one of my file clerks here. As soon as I heard her story, however, I retired her with full pay. With the understanding, of course, that she not spread this unsavory tale."

"Of course," Manning said. For the next several minutes he gave voice to the more salient aspects of J. Barnaby's character. When he finally stopped, it was only because he ran out of breath.

"Purely one man's opinion," J. Barnaby said loftily. He gazed lovingly at the photograph in his hand. "When will you be ready to leave for Mizar, my dear boy?"

"Oh, I'll go," Manning said sourly. "You haven't left me any choice. I'll go at, once—the quicker I can get away from the same planet you're on, the better. I'll like it. But I'll find some way to make you pay for this, if it's the last thing I do."

"I've already ordered an encyclotape on Mizar to be put on your ship," J. Barnaby said. He put the photograph away in his desk with an air of regret. "You will go to Mizar as Cultural Attaché of the Planet Department. Your job is to stop the Acruxian in whatever he's doing, but to do it in such a way there will be no interplanetary incidents. By the way, what I said about giving you a concession still goes. If there's one you want, clear it with me. So long as it isn't something that some cabinet member wants, you can have it."

"That means if it's worthless," Manning grunted. "I can't see them passing up anything that's any good."

"The minute you can assure me the job's done," J. Barnaby continued, "call me here and you can watch me destroy this evidence. Have a good trip, son."

Manning glared at his father-in-law and left.

WHEN HE ARRIVED at the government port, he found the ship free of guards. He climbed in and blasted off, sending the ship hurtling away from Rigil Kentaurus with all the speed he could give her.

When he was finally well beyond the last patrol ring, he fed the coordinates of Mizar I into the ship and threw her into magnidrive. Then he put in a call to Vega and explained that J. Barnaby had tricked him into another government mission, without bothering to go into details as to how this had been done. By the time he'd finished talking to her, and listened to the babbling of his small son, he was more resigned to the job ahead. He found the encyclotape on Mizar and slipped it into the audio-reader. Then he leaned back to listen.

"Mizar I," said a pleasant voice from the concealed speaker, "is a Class B planet in the double-star system of Mizar. It is expected to be admitted to the Federation early in 3474. The planet is a mean distance from its sun of ninety-four million miles. Its mass is 0.8 in relation to that of Terra; its volume, 0.8992; its density is 5.12 times that of water; its diameter, six thousand three hundred miles; orbital velocity, 17.2 miles per second; escape velocity, 6.2 miles per second; period of rotation, twenty-four hours, fifty-eight minutes; eccentricity, 0.0123—"

Manning Draco reached over and punched a button, The tape skipped a few inches and the voice took up its story again.

"—gravity at surface, 0.92. More than ninety percent of the surface of Mizar I is under water and consequently the civilization is an underwater one. The dominant race on Mizar is evolved from an oviparous form of life similar to the *Ornithorynchus anatinus,* once found on Terra, which was at home both in and out of water. They have constructed great underwater cities, protected from water by synthetic bubbles and supplied with fresh air which is extracted from the surrounding water. In general form, the Mizarians are humanoid, although their facial features are quite different from that of Terrans. While they have not advanced industrially to a point where they are on a par with the more advanced races of the galaxy, they have surpassed most races in underwater agriculture and in the extraction of food and minerals from water. Politically, Mizar is an empire and the present ruler is Emperor Alis Volat. There is also a parliament which is elected every two years. The most striking thing about the Mizarians is that as a race they are cryptesthesists. It is believed that this has been their chief natural defense and explains why they have never been successfully invaded.

"The male Mizarians still retain a horny organ on the heel pleach foot, in appearance somewhat like a natural spur, which was a characteristic of their primitive ancestors and was not lost in the evolutionary process. This organ is connected with poison glands and is still capable of functioning in the modern Mizarian. In recent times, however, the Mizarians have taken to wearing shoes, mostly as a sign of friendly intentions, much as the Achernarians will often wear fashionable rear-aprons to indicate that they don't intend to use their rudimentary sting-ers. Certain sociologists have also related this to the Terran custom of—"

Manning reached over and snapped the machine off.

"—shaking hands with their right hands to show that no weapon is being held in it," continued a pleasantly soft voice.

Manning started to turn off the machine again, then realized the switch was already at the off position. When that fact had penetrated, he whirled to look behind him.

SHE STOOD in the doorway to the galley in the rear of the ship. She was a tiny thing, no more than four feet tall, but quite obviously a perfectly formed humanoid female. Her light blue hair swirled down around her shoulders, making a perfect frame for the tiny, golden-tanned face. Even at that distance, he could see that her eyes were a bright orange. A soft white scarf was wound fully around her neck, then fell down between her bare breasts to her waist. A thin, jeweled thong circled her waist and from it another white scarf hung to the floor. Her neck was fully covered, as were approximately three inches in the middle of her body, but for the rest she was bare. It was a figure that any Terran woman might have been proud to possess.

"Who the hell are you?" Manning demanded when he had recovered enough to talk.

"Nisa Brioshe," she answered. She smiled, inclining her head, and he saw that there was another narrow thong running over the top of her hair and down to the very tip of her nose. It was covered with tiny flashing jewels. "At your service."

Dressed as she was, he wasn't sure what the "service" meant and decided it was better not to ask. "What are you doing on my ship?" he asked.

"You are a Terran, aren't you?" she asked.

Manning nodded.

"Returning to Terra?" she continued.

"Not now," he said. "I'm heading for Mizar. We'll be there, in fact, in another hour."

For a moment, she looked disappointed. Then her face brightened. "But you will return to Terra after you have completed your visit to Mizar?"

"Yes," Manning said, "but what does that have to do with your being here on my ship?"

"Everything," she said simply. "It is necessary that I go to Terra for a short time. I had managed to get as far as Rigil Kentaurus and yours seemed to be the first ship going from there to Terra. So I came aboard the first time the guards were not looking."

Manning cursed under his breath. It was bad enough that he had to make this trip to Mizar without his life being complicated by the presence of a stowaway—especially one who was so good-looking and so obviously female. Yet it was his own fault. He should have discovered her presence before he even left Rigil Kentaurus[14] and he would have if he hadn't been too angry to check his ship properly.

"Can't you cover yourself up more?" he asked.

"Why?" she responded, looking down at herself. "It displeases you?"

---

14 The *Alpha Actuary* had a spy ray which would analyze and identify almost anything, animate or inanimate, which might be on the ship, but Manning had neglected to check it.

"N-no," Manning said truthfully, "but it is disconcerting."

She laughed. "You are the first Terran with whom I have talked. I like you. How are you called on Terra?"

"Manning Draco."

"Manning Draco?" she repeated. She spoke the language well, yet there was an exotic way to her pronunciation of his name. "It is a pleasing sound. Did I tell you that I am called Nisa Brioshe?"

"You did," Manning said dryly. "Where are you from? I don't recall any blue-haired, orange-eyed humanoids in the Federation."

"We are not a part of the Federation, Manning Draco. I am from Rasalague."

"Acruxian Axis?"

She shook her head until the blue hair danced on her shoulders. "We are an independent system. We carry on a certain amount of trade with both the Acruxians and your Federation. The amount depends entirely upon who comes to trade with us, since we have no spaceships of our own."

"Why do you have to go to Terra?" Manning asked.

"It is my time," she said. She smiled at his bewilderment. "We have migratory mating habits. Once this was confined to our own planet, but now when it is time for a Rasalaguan to mate she is assigned to another world. I have been ordered to Terra. Now that I've met you, I'm glad."

"Look," Manning said hastily, "maybe there are a few things you should know about Terra. We are a monogamous society—or at least that's the general idea even though most Terrans ignore it—and I am happily married. That means that I have a mate already, and I don't think she'd like it if I took part in any migratory mating games."

She laughed again. "I like you," she announced.

TO MANNING, her laughter had a faintly ominous ring. He decided to shift the conversation to safer ground. At the same time, he tried to ignore the way she was dressed, or rather the way she wasn't dressed. "How do you manage these migrations since you have no spaceships?" he asked.

"Like this," she said. "We avail ourselves of other ships!"

"A whole planet full of stowaways!" exclaimed Manning. "If the Department of Transportation ever finds out about this they'll be hysterical. Nisa, my sweet, you represent a problem...."

She arched her eyebrows. "A problem? I was assured that my appearance would be pleasing to most Terrans and that the only problem might be one of controlling interested Terran males."

"I was thinking of a different problem," Manning said quickly. "I meant I can hardly take you back to Rigil Kentaurus now. Even if I could, it might mean trouble for both of us. As a matter of fact, I can't imagine how you got there without being discovered. They're pretty touchy about strangers landing there."

She giggled. "I arrived on the private ship of a—I believe he said he was a senator. He is expecting me to visit him tonight."

"I'm beginning to understand," Manning said dryly, with another look at her figure. "Well, you're still a problem. I don't mind your riding to Terra with me, but I have certain work to do on Mizar before then."

"That is no problem, Manning. I will not interfere with your work. I will merely stay with you and keep out of the way when you are working."

There didn't seem to be much choice for Manning. He couldn't take her back and he couldn't just abandon her out in space. He tried to make the best of an awkward situation. "We'll be friends," he said. "You understand? Friends. Then when we do get to Terra, perhaps I can introduce you to some nice, unattached young men."

She gave him a long look from beneath lowered lashes. "I think we will be very good friends," she said. It was impossible to tell whether she was putting special emphasis on any of the words.

Manning shuddered and pretended to find it necessary to give attention to the ship. If there was a slight crackling sound in his ears, it undoubtedly came from the thin ice on which he felt he was treading. On top of the phony blackmail material his father-in-law already had, this was all he needed.

The ship shortly came out of magnidrive and hovered over the planet of Mizar I. Gazing into the landing screen, Manning could see almost nothing but oceans. He switched on his communicator and soon contacted someone on Mizar. He identified himself and was given instructions for bringing the ship down on a small island which had been converted into a spaceport. He was told that a subtaxi would come there to pick him up.

He followed a landing beam down to the spaceport and then guided the ship into a parking cradle and shut off the power.

"Let's go," he said, sounding more cheerful than he felt.

He and the girl went through the air-lock and stepped out on the spaceport. They were already near what was obviously a small dock and there was a sign in Terran and several other languages, announcing that this was a taxi station.

"I forgot something," Manning said suddenly. "You stay here and I'll be right back. There should be someone along any minute to pick us up."

He turned and hurried back into the ship. There, he looked quickly through the encyclotape index and found one on Rasalague. He put it in the audio-reader and snapped it on. He sent the reader skipping along the tape until he found a reference to Rasalague mating habits. Then he listened.

"...Almost nothing is known about the sex and mating, habits of the Rasalaguans," the voice said. "Any number of surveys have been made but the Rasalaguans refuse to answer any direct questions. A number of facts, however, have been observed which have in turn led to several theories. For one thing, there are no males on the planet. On at least twenty occasions, Terran observers have been present at the birth of Rasalaguan young and they were also all female. It is known that when a Rasalaguan is considered ready for mating, she is sent away. She invariably returns within a few months and shortly after her return her children are born. Nothing is known about the method of conception or who the father is. This has impelled one authority, Dr. Hans Boichik, to advance the theory that Rasalaguans always mate with a male of another species, while Dr. Anna Maidele—"

Manning had heard enough and none of it was reassuring. He turned the machine off and went outside again. The subtaxi was just arriving as he rejoined Nisa Brioshe.

CHAPTER THREE

THE SUBTAXI looked somewhat like an old-fashioned Terran submarine. A door in the top swung open and Manning and Nisa stepped inside. There, they found themselves facing the first Mizarian that Manning had ever seen. It was a rather startling sight.

The Mizarian, although he was sitting down, looked to be almost six feet tall. The lower part of his body was encased in clothing similar to Terran trousers and he wore shoes which seemed to be made of light suede. The upper part of his body was bare, but was covered with dark, feather-like hair—or hair-like feathers, it was difficult to tell which. Two powerful arms terminated in four-fingered hands that looked as if they had evolved from front feet. The general outlines of his body and head were certainly humanoid, but his face still resembled that of his primitive ancestor. The top and sides of his head were covered with the same hair-feathers that were on his body and he was apparently equipped only with internal ears. He had two small eyes and then the rest of his face protruded in a large duckbill, with nostril holes in the top of the bill. When he smiled. Manning saw that the inside of his bill was filled with horny plates rather than teeth.[15]

---

15 As the encyclotape had informed Manning, Mizarians were descended from the *Ornithorynchus anatinus*, better known on Terra as the Duckbill Platypus. (On Terra, they dated from the Mesozoic era, and in an evolutionary sense never progressed beyond that era.) In their primitive stage on Mizar, they had been similar

The door of the subtaxi closed as soon as they were inside. It submerged immediately and started down through the ocean. When it was under way, Manning discovered that there were windows in the sides of the taxi so they could took out.

At first there was nothing to see but water and a few fish which were fairly similar to those found on Terra. But as they went lower, he began to notice patches of algae of various colors. These patches seemed unusually uniform and, finally as they passed one especially large patch, he commented upon it.

"Yes, sir," their driver said. "As a matter of fact, that was one of the finest bacillariophyceae farms on Mizar. Belongs to the Emperor—although, of course, he doesn't farm it himself."

Manning's surprise vanished as he realized it was probably logical for an underwater civilization to farm algae. "Is that your chief crop?" he asked.

"One of the chief crops," the driver said. "Of course, there are several types. Some people prefer cyandphyceae, some chlorophyceae, some phaeophyceae, and so on."

"Any other sort of farms?" Manning asked.

The driver gestured through the window where they could see some small craft rounding up a school of whales. "We're just passing one of the largest dairy farms," he said.

As they went deeper, Manning noticed the various levels of coral. It seemed almost too beautiful to have grown in that fashion. He asked the driver about it.

"Yes, sir, this approach to the city is all coralscaped. We've been controlling the growth and life cycle of coral for many generations. I understand that you Terrans also control the natural growth of your planet to make it more beautiful."

"Not only that," Manning said. "We have also learned how

---

to the Terran form. They had lived mostly in the water, with their nests in tunnels up out of the water. This ability to live both in and out of water may account for their having become the dominant race on ocean-covered Mizar. The evolved race was still nocturnal, as had been their ancestors, and they still hatched their young from eggs, the mothers nursing the young once they were out of the shells.

to conceal it behind various kinds of advertising. That's another step of culture which you will undoubtedly learn in time."

Within a few more minutes, the sub taxi neared the city. Manning could see it ahead of them as they dived. There was something weirdly beautiful about coming upon a sprawling city beneath a transparent bubble far below the surface of the ocean.

The taxi entered a waterlock and they waited until the water had drained out. Then, moving on wheels, the taxi entered the main bubble. There it stopped and the driver indicated that this was as far as he went.

AS THEY STEPPED from the taxi, there was another Mizarian waiting for them. He also wore a single garment, but there was a bright red sash angling across his chest. It seemed to be more a badge of caste than a garment and Manning later learned that this was correct.

"Mr. Draco?" the Mizarian asked. His manner was tinged with the faint hostility which Manning was to find among most of the Mizarians.

"Yes," Manning said.

"I am Depro Fundis, equerry to his Royal Mostness, Emperor Alis Volat. It is my duty to meet such individuals as your Planet Department wishes to send to us. I understood, however, that you would be alone. Is this, perhaps, your consort?"

"No," Manning said. "This is Miss Nisa Brioshe, a friend of mine."

"Friend?" the Mizarian asked. His face was expressionless, but his tone made up for it.

"Friend," Manning said firmly. "She will stay wherever I do, but in a separate room. Is that clear?"

"As clear as most of the things you Terrans do," the equerry said coldly. "It will be as you wish. We try to be tolerant of the fetishes of other races. Come. I have a vehicle waiting."

He led the way to an egg-shaped ground vehicle. He held

the door open for them, then followed them inside. He gave the driver an order in his own language, then settled back, making a point of not sitting any closer to them than necrssary.

"You are fortunate," he said, "in that you arrive on Mizar in the middle of our most important Egg Festival. It is a holiday which I imagine to be unsurpassed in your own world, so it should give you pleasure, in addition to serving your official purpose. You are here as a cultural observer, are you not?"

Manning nodded.

"I can understand your desire to observe our culture, but I really don't understand what good it will do you. Since you aren't even oviparous, it is doubtful if you can understand it."

Manning was beginning to be annoyed by the attitude. "Oh, I don't know," he said. "We may not be oviparous, but you can't say we don't know anything about eggs. Why, we Terrans make the best omelets in the universe."

The flesh around the Mizarian's bill paled visibly. "That was a rather crude remark," he said frigidly. "It might be interpreted as proving the ideas of some of our people."[16]

"Maybe," Manning grunted. "Where are we going now?"

"I shall take you to your hotel. We have reserved quarters there for you and I presume you can manage to get additional quarters for your—friend. I'm afraid that I must then return to the palace, but we have arranged for someone to escort you to the Festival. He should arrive shortly after we do."

"I hope he will be in better humor than you are," Manning said.

---

16 There was a small political group on Mizar which contended that Terrans— and all other races that were egg-eating—were cannibals and therefore to be regarded only with suspicion and horror. A popular Mizarian psychologist had even managed to get possession of a museum copy of Jonathan Swift and had used it to prove that Terran literature was filled with a sadistic attitude toward eggs. He was particularly concerned over a dish he interpreted as Freud Eggs. He had quite an elaborate theory about the oviphobia of Terrans being derived from a profound sense of loss in discovering that they were not hatched out of eggs. It is too large a subject to cover here, but those who are interested might look up his two books— *The Egg and You* and *Ovum Dentata* by Dr. Par Egzanpl.

For some reason this seemed to amuse the Mizarian. He gave a short laugh, which bore a slight resemblance to quacking.

"What's the joke?" Manning asked. "Or maybe, I should say what's the yolk?"

The offended equerry refused to speak for the rest of the journey.

SHORTLY AFTER delivering them at the hotel, the equerry left. Manning arranged with the clerk for Nisa Brioshe to have a room on a different floor, but on her insistence it was changed to the room right next to his.

Manning's sense of security was further shattered by Nisa insisting that the connecting door be left open. His experience with his father-in-law had left him in such a nervous state that he kept expecting to have photographers leap out from behind every potted seaweed. Every time Nisa drew near, he was careful to move farther away, so that at times their conversations bore a striking resemblance to a chase scene off the visiscreen.

Actually Nisa Brioshe was exhibiting no more than the friendliness she had professed, but her costume was so filled (as it were) with lustier promises it was difficult not to leap to plenty of other conclusions.

They had been in the hotel room—singular because Nisa had spent all of the intervening time in his room—for less than an hour when there was a knock on the door. Manning, still thinking of photographers, tried to get Nisa to retreat to her own room, but was unsuccessful. As the rappings of the visitor began to sound impatient, he finally gave up.

"Come in," he called.

The door swung slowly open and the visitor stepped inside.

Manning Draco stared in complete astonishment.

The newcomer was not a Mizarian. He was at least seven feet tall, his huge cylindrical body was supported by three thick legs. His body was dark gray and bare except for a green, fringed skirt. A holster carried a three-barreled weapon. His head was a pale red knob, perfectly smooth except for a mouth opening and the two inverted ears, covered with a fine network of hairs. Two eye-stalks reared up from the top of his head. He had four tentacles, now weaving with pleasure, two at waist level and two at shoulder level.

It was now about five months, at least, since Manning had lasts seen Dtilla Raishelle, the chief agent provocateur for Acrux.

"You!" Manning said. "What are you doing here?"

"Is that the way to greet an old friend?" the Acruxian asked with mock sadness. "Here I've been rehearsing pretty speeches to make to you, and you insist on starting off on such an unfriendly basis. Who's your pretty friend? I hope I didn't interrupt anything."

"No, you didn't interrupt anything," Manning said savagely. Why, he wondered to himself, couldn't anyone accept the fact that he was happily married and through with prowling. "Nisa, this unsavory-looking visitor is Dtilla Raishelle, an Acruxian spy. Miss Brioshe is from Rasalague."

If Manning had been watching closely, he might have noticed that Dtilla Raishelle seemed momentarily disturbed by this.

"What is she doing here?" he asked.

"She's on her way to Terra," Manning said shortly. "She's merely going there with me when I leave. And that's all."

"Then it is a pleasure to meet her," Dtilla said with a courtly bow. "May I inquire if you are ready?"

"Ready for what?" Manning wanted to know.

"You haven't been informed?" Dtilla asked. His tentacles were once more waving with pleasure. "During the important Egg Festival on Mizar, it is traditional to give temporary appointments to aliens who may be on the planet—I imagine you yourself will be given one in a day or two. But I have been appointed a Royal Host of Mizar and am here to escort you to the Festival."

Manning looked at him with suspicion. "What if I don't want to go to any Festival?" he asked.

"That is your privilege, of course," the Acruxian said. "But may I take the liberty of pointing out that the Mizarians will be deeply offended. Considering the present state of feeling here concerning the Federation and Terrans, it would be most unwise for one who is presumably here as a sort of diplomat."

Against his will, Manning agreed. As a matter of fact, he hadn't intended to refuse; he'd merely been expressing some of the annoyance he was feeling. But he certainly had no intention of passing up the chance to spend as much time in the company of Dtilla Raishelle as he could. There would probably be no quicker way of finding out what the Acruxian was up to.

He wanted to leave Nisa in the hotel, but she looked so disappointed at the suggestion that he relented.

"By the way, my dear friend," Dtilla said as the three of them left the hotel, "I'm sure you won't mind a bit of frankness on my part. When we last met on Regulus, I fear that I was not familiar with the special qualities of the great Manning Draco. As a result, you were able to trick me in a most ignoble fashion. Since then, however, I have corrected the state of my ignorance and the situation will now be quite different."

"Maybe," Manning grunted. "What are you doing here—or, rather, what do you claim is your legitimate reason for being here?"

"Both are the same," the Acruxian said. "I am here as an official representative of my government. My function is merely to act in a friendly fashion to the Mizarians, so that they will not be unduly influenced by the vicious Federation propaganda about us."

"Yeah?" Manning said. "Dtilla, you should write a book called 'How to Win Friends and Influence Mizarians.' It would probably be a best-seller in the light fiction class."

CHAPTER FOUR

DTILLA RAISHELLE was driving an official ground vehicle and he took them quickly across town to the area that had been turned over to the Festival. It was a section which normally was a park, probably fifty acres in size. At first glance, it seemed almost like a festival ground on Terra. Various types of temporary buildings had been erected, most of them made out of cheap plastic in various bright colors. Most of them were also influenced in design by either the egg or the nest. Manning had noticed the same influence in the more permanent architecture as they had driven through the city streets.

These temporary buildings housed a great variety of games and exhibits. When he stopped to examine the games closely, Manning discovered they were completely alien and yet there was something familiar about them, as though it were impossible for any festival anywhere to be very different from all other festivals. There was even a large stadium with a well-turfed center which might have been meant to be a playing field.

"Egg contest," Dtilla explained when he asked about it. "The climax of this whole affair."

"Egg contest?"

"Yeah. Every mother brings her unhatched eggs here on the final day of the Festival and a judge decides which is the most beautiful egg."[17]

There were also a great variety of rides, most of these being underwater, but except for that difference they might well have originated on Terra. Then Manning caught sight of a building which was even more familiar. He stopped and stared at the sign which was over the entrance—a sign which was prepared in several languages.

MYSTO THE GREAT

Know what the future holds in store for you! Now for the first time on Mizar, Mysto the Great is available to tell you of the events which are yet to come! Mysto the Great sees all! Mysto the Great knows all! Mysto the Great tells all! Exclusive seer to his Royal Mostness, Emperor Alis Volat!

"A fortune teller," Manning exclaimed.

"Something like that," Dtilla Raishelle said. "Now over here, we have—" He went on explaining how one of the games worked, but Manning paid no attention. He was more interested in the idea of a Mizarian fortune teller.

---

17 Basically, as Manning had observed to himself, things were not so different here. He even discovered later that there was a popular Mizarian song which was called "I'll Bet You Were a Beautiful Egg."

It was certainly doing more business than any other building on the grounds. There was a steady stream of Mizarians going in and out of the building of Mysto the Great.

After a time, Manning noticed something else. Any number of Mizarians brushed by him on their way into the fortune teller's and paid absolutely no attention to him. Yet invariably the same Mizarians, on exiting, would look at him with hostility. Some of them even muttered under their breaths, while others went so far as to clack their bills angrily as they strode past him. His curiosity began to be more than idle.

"Just a minute." he said when Dtilla finally tried to lead them to another part of the grounds. "I think I'd like to have my fortune told."

"That is a foolishness for children," the Acruxian said waspishly. "Now, if you'll come along with, me, I'll show you one of the most interesting sights here. Right over there they have a collection of—"

"Later, Buster," Manning interrupted. "Right now I want to have my fortune told."

"It is a waste of time," grumbled Dtilla. "We should have to wait in line and besides, the Mizarians might resent it if three aliens were to intrude on such a popular booth."

KNOWING THAT it was probably a waste of time, Manning Draco still tried a lightning mental stab at the Acruxian. As he had expected, Dtilla's secondary shield was too strong, for him—but even so he caught a brief impression of unease before the shield locked into place. It was all he had been looking for and he felt satisfied. Especially so when Dtilla gave him a reproachful look.

"I hate show-offs," the Acruxian announced. "I am well aware that you are the only Terran with a secondary mind shield and that you have far more telepathic power than anyone on your planet, but I must say it's a little childish of you to do that. And hopeless."

"Is it?" Manning asked. He grinned, his good spirits suddenly restored. "Come on, my fine Acruxian, I am going to have my fortune told."

"But—"

"I insist," Manning said firmly.

"Wouldn't you like your fortune told, Nisa?"

"I already know my fortune," she said, "but it might be nice to listen to yours."

Dtilla Raishelle shrugged and followed the two of them into the line before the building.

When they finally reached the entrance, the three of them entered together. Manning had already anticipated something of the sort, so he was not surprised when the Acruxian cried out as they entered the dimly lighted room.

"Mysto the Great, I, a Royal Host, bring you a most distinguished and famous guest from a far-off planet, one who in his way is famous throughout the galaxy as Manning Draco."

Manning grinned and knew he was on the right track. He was beginning to enjoy himself.

"Enter—and welcome," said a muffled voice.

Mysto the Great sat behind a large table on which a number of cards were placed in such a manner that he could see them but his visitor could not. In the dim light, his bulky figure could be seen, but that was about all. Some sort of white robe covered him so completely that no part of the seer could be seen.

As he sat down on the other side of the table, Manning tried a mental probe of the figure in front of him. He came up against a blank wall which he recognized as a shield and not the natural mental block which the Mizarians possessed.

"What is it you wish?" the muffled voice asked.

"You're a fortune teller," Manning said casually. "Why don't you just go ahead and tell me."

There was a pause, then the voice, spoke again from behind the layers of cloth. "Know you, O Terran, that certain arts of fortune telling—*l'art de tirer les cartes*—is reserved for the Sons of the Doctrine and that only I, Mysto the Great, hold the Key to the Mysteries of the Universe.

"From the cards I see that your life is dominated by the Magus, or Juggler, the caster of the dice and mountebank, in the world of vulgar trickery. The Magus, which is of the Greater Arcana, signifies that unity which is the mother of numbers and—"

Before anyone could guess what he was doing, Manning reached over and grabbed one of the cards. He turned the face and looked at it. It showed a heavily robed young man standing behind a table. Above his head was the symbol of infinity, looking like the figure in a horizontal position. On the table in front of him were a pentacle, a sword, a cup, and a staff. Flowers and vines grew around the legs of the table.

"I thought that sounded a little familiar," Manning said. "Now what sort of a Mizarian fortune teller would use cards which originated on Terra and were once known as the Tarot?"

"You," the muffled voice exclaimed angrily, "have defiled the sacred presence. I will not—"

Manning leaned forward quickly, grabbed a handful of the white cloth, and yanked on it. It had been wrapped on carelessly, and quickly, and the whole robe came away in his hand. For the second time that day Manning. Draco found himself gazing on a familiar countenance. But this one was even more familiar.

The fortune teller was a certain Rigelian known as Dzanku Dzanku.

"That tears it," Dzanku said and stood up.

THERE WERE CERTAIN similarities between Dzanku and the Acruxian. Dzanku was shorter, being only a few inches over six feet tall. His thick, square torso was supported by only two tree-like legs, but in the matter of tentacles he was two up on the Acruxian, having a total of six. His face, the same grayish color as his body, was small and devoid of expression. Three eye-stalks loomed over the top of his face.

"Manning, old friend," he said. "I can't tell you what a surprise it is to see you. It must be eight or nine months since we last met—although, truthfully, it seems like only yesterday."

"What are you doing here?" Manning demanded.

"Just trying to turn an honest credit or two," Dzanku said innocently. One of his eye-stalks swiveled in the direction of Nisa Brioshe. "Ah, Manning, you sly dog you! I see you are up to your old tricks. You always did have an eye for a good-looking female—although I must admit I thought you might reform after your marriage."

"This is Nisa Brioshe, *a friend*," Manning said coldly.

"Miss Brioshe is from Rasalague," Dtilla put in, "but she just happens to be along with Manning. On her way to Terra. I understand."

"I am charmed," Dzanku said. He inclined all three of his eye-stalks toward her. "My name is Dzanku Dzanku, since our friend Manning is too ill-mannered to introduce us. I regret that I am not more humanoid in form or I would make Manning more aware of what a charming—ah—*friend* he has."

"Enough of this," Manning cut in. "I still want to know what you're doing here. It's almost nine months since I sent you and Sam Warren and Pisha Paisha to the first planet in the system of Caph.[18] It should have taken you at least fifty or a hundred years to escape from there and even so the patrol should have caught you on the way out."

"It was clever of you," Dzanku admitted, "but not quite clever enough. I fear, my dear Manning, that the flaw in your reasoning was that you based everything on the fact that the Caphians on the first planet had never gone in for interplanetary travel."

"You mean they had?"

---

18   See "The Caphian Caper." Caph I is in a Time Fracture which so distorts time in relation to the rest of the galaxy that while a week passed on Caph I five years would go by in the outside universe. Knowing that Caph I had never developed spaceships, Manning had Dzanku there with barely enough fuel to reach the planet. He had felt certain it would take at least two months, or fifty years galaxy time, for Dzanku to escape.

"No, but the only reason they hadn't was that they didn't have any desire to do so. They like their own planet and don't have any desire to meet other worlds. You might call it a bucolic attitude, but they're quite happy about the whole thing. They have, however, a very efficient fission power which they use industrially. You wouldn't be interested in all the sordid details, but they were quite happy to help me convert it to use in the ship in which I arrived. By pushing ourselves, it took only twenty-two hours from the time we landed until we were ready to leave.[19] So only eight months had passed by the time we left the Time Fracture. As for the patrol, it was a simple matter to dodge them." He waved his tentacles modestly.

"And I suppose," Manning said dryly, "it's merely a coincidence that you and Dtilla Raishelle both show up here and that you both were anxious for me not to know you were present?"

"Of course, dear fellow," the Acruxian said.

DZANKU DZANKU stared speculatively at Manning out of his three eyes. "You know, cousin," he said, speaking to Dtilla, "Manning and I have known each other a long time and upon a few occasions have been rather close. I have a very high opinion of his ability. I think that under the circumstances we might be perfectly frank with him."

"As you think, cousin," Dtilla replied. Neither Dzanku nor Dtilla was using this term loosely since the two races are

---

19 As it was later learned, Caph I had managed to discover two new atomic elements unknown in the rest of the galaxy. They had also invented their own version of the Fermi-egg. Briefly, they put the nuclei of Arcturium-216 (123 on the atomic table) in their Caphotron and when its neutrons are captured by the A-229 isotope, the resulting nuclei are inherently unstable and, emitting two electrons one after another, are transformed into the nuclei of two new elements known as Alphardonium and Spicanium, atomic numbers 147 and 148. If there are any amateur scientists in the audience who would like to manufacture their own Alphardonium, the formula is as follows:

$$_{92}A^{216} + on^1 - \rightarrow {}_{92}As^{217} + \text{radiation}$$
$$_{92}A^{217} - \rightarrow {}_{93}As^{217} + e$$
$$_{93}As^{217} - \rightarrow {}_{94}Sp^{217} + e$$

And that's all there is to it. However, the use of the Fermi-egg is not to be confused with that of the more popular hen's egg.

related—Acruxians being, in a manner of speaking, sport model Rigelians.

"Hold on to your scarves, honey," Manning said in an aside to Nisa. "When Dzanku Dzanku decides to be frank, it's time for honest folk to head for a storm cellar."

"Manning, you wound me deeply," Dzanku said. "I presume you are aware of the rather peculiar talent which Mizarians possess?"

Manning nodded.

"Actually," Dzanku continued, "it's always been a rather useless talent. Oh, very handy in such things as chess, checkers. Castorian Rummy, and possibly Tzitsa, if they were only clever enough to play it—and, of course, as you Terrans were quick to realize, it is an ability which would be most valuable in pilots of fighting ships. But all it has meant to the Mizarians is some mild amusement, something to while away a long, dull day. I presume that once it served them a purpose in their days of hand-to-hand fighting, but this is all it has meant to them for many generations. Being such a limited talent, however, it has created in them the desire for more of the same. If you were to study Mizarian history, you would discover that they wasted much of their time trying out all forms of fortune telling. This brings us up to me and my use of what you so astutely recognized as ancient Terran Tarot cards."

"I wondered if we were going to get around to that," Manning murmured.

"As you know," Dzanku continued blandly, "my good cousin is interested in furthering his own aims as opposed to those of the Federation. Since Mizar has been about to join the Federation, he did not want to break any laws in trying to convince the Mizarians that this was not in their best interests. So he is here, being merely the good friend which he is. And I am doing a rather rousing business as a fortune teller—I'm really quite good at it—specializing in pointing out the future as it will be if the Mizarians permit themselves to become a part of a

Federation dominated by Terrans. This is a rather easy matter for me since I have had considerable contact with Terrans."

"Most of the time to the Terrans' sorrow," Manning observed. "So you are responsible for the anti-Federation feeling that is growing here?"

"I like to think that I have at least nurtured it," Dzanku said with pride. "I understand, my dear Manning, that you are no longer an insurance investigator, but are now representing the Federation, so I would like to point out there is nothing illegal in my activity, as distasteful as you may find it. As I said before, I am merely turning an honest credit or so."

"That's an implausible idea if I ever heard one," Manning said.

"I give you my word," said Dzanku solemnly. "I have learned that the life of crime is a path beset with thorns and stones—not precious stones, I hasten to add. I have determined to rehabilitate myself as a useful member of society. I am thinking of writing my memoirs so that the young and impressionable may benefit by my horrible example. In fact, I was intending to dedicate it to Manning Draco—the man who taught me that crime doesn't pay."

"Very touching," Manning said dryly. "By the way, where is Sam Warren?"

"Sam?" Dzanku said. "Good old Sam? Why, I haven't seen him since—"

This ringing declaration was ruined by the sudden opening of a door back of Dzanku. A rather slight Terran, with a shrewd face, burst into the room. He was easily recognized as the Terran who had so long worked with the Rigelian.

"Dzanku," he cried, "I've just learned that Manning—" He broke off as he caught sight of the others in the room.

Manning laughed. "Since you haven't seen Sam in such a long time," he said, "I wouldn't think of intruding on what I am sure will be a tender reunion. I'll see you boys around. Come on, Nisa."

With the pretty little Rasalaguan following him, Manning left the building. They walked past the long line of glowering Mizarians who were waiting to have their futures foretold. After a number of inquiries and several rebuffs, they finally found a public vehicle which would return them to the hotel.

On the way, without completely revealing his own mission, Manning told Nisa about Dzanku, Sam, and Dtilla Raishelle. The mere fact that Dzanku had been trying to conceal Sam Warren's presence was enough to prove that they had some scheme other than the one they had revealed so frankly, but Manning couldn't guess what it might be. Actually, he was merely talking aloud more than telling her, but she hung on his every word.

Back at the hotel, it was with some difficulty that he finally persuaded Nisa that she should retire to her own room. Then he made certain that the connecting door was locked, propped a chair up against it, and with a wry smile—for the situation of Manning Draco trying to protect himself from an ardent female was indeed a switch—went to bed.

CHAPTER FIVE

MANNING WAS UP early the following morning. He'd already decided his first step would be to try to see the Emperor. He had intended to slip out before Nisa was up, but she must have heard him moving around in the room, for she knocked on the connecting door almost as soon as he was up.

They had breakfast served in Manning's room. Nisa was dressed in the same scanty costume she had worn the day before and there were times when Manning, sitting across from her, found it difficult to concentrate on eating. Although it was an age when women dressed lightly throughout the galaxy, Rasalaguans went a little farther in this direction than any other peoples.[20]

---

20 There were many people who considered this pretty brazen of the Rasala-

They had barely finished breakfast when there was a knock on the door.

"Come in," Manning called.

The door opened and a Mizarian entered. It was the royal equerry who had met them the day before. From the expression on his face, it was quite obvious he didn't feel any friendlier than he had the first time.

"Terran Manning Draco," he said, "it is the wish of his Royal Mostness, Emperor Alis Volat, that you be given the honor of being the Royal Egg Judge for the duration of the Festival. Although the chief egg contest will take place on the last day of the Festival, there will be a number of sub-egg contests before, starting with today. In each case, it will be your duty to judge which is the most beautiful egg."

"I appreciate the honor," Manning said solemnly, knowing that to him one egg had always looked like another. "By the way, I'd like to apologize for anything I may have said yesterday which gave offense." He'd decided he had better try to repair his diplomatic bridges. The equerry acted as if he hadn't heard the apology. "His Royal Mostness also requests your presence at the Royal Palace. At once."

"Fine," Manning said. "I was about to request an audience with Emperor Alis Volat. Nisa, you'll have to stay here until I return."

"All right, Manning," she said submissively.

The equerry drove him to the palace. He answered briefly any questions Manning put to him, but otherwise discouraged conversation. When they arrived at the palace—a huge edifice

---

guans, but actually they were a highly moral race. It was eventually learned that in terms of their own culture and their biological make-up the Rasalaguans dressed far more modestly than any other race. Due to the Terran way of looking at such things, however, there was a period when visiscreen producers and advertisers tried to find ways of working a Rasalaguan into every story and every ad in order to have an excuse for showing one of these charming females. Their efforts came to nothing, as the Rasalaguans refused to be photographed under any conditions. This explains why so few Terrans were familiar with Rasalaguans.

built in the shape of an egg—he drove past the front entrance and around to the rear.

"It is thought wiser if you go in the back way," he explained. "As you may have discovered, many Mizarian subjects do not feel too friendly to Terrans. It might create disturbances if it were known that His Mostness was receiving a Terran."

"Won't they also object to my being an egg judge?" Manning asked.

"No. It is realized that visitors must be given such honors. And of course if you show an aptitude for judging eggs, that may mitigate some of the feeling about you."

HE PARKED the land vehicle near the rear entrance and they got out. They had to pick their way through a number of large cans, resembling Terran garbage cans. Because of the similarity, Manning assumed that's what they were until he happened to look in one of the cans. It was filled to the top with what appeared to be gold dust. He stopped and scooped up a handful. It *was* gold dust.

"What's this?" he asked in amazement.

The equerry glanced briefly at the can. "Garbage," he said.

"What?"

"Garbage," the equerry repeated patiently.

"Royal-type garbage?" Manning asked dryly.

"All of our garbage is gold," the Mizarian said coldly.

"Why?" Manning asked. "Fillings drop out of your teeth while you're eating, or something like that?"

"Mizarians," the equerry explained, "have teeth only when they are very young. The teeth then wear out and are replaced by the horny plates of the adult."

"How does that explain the gold garbage?"

"Our food is essentially the same as it was for our ancestors—various succulent insects, shellfish, and perhaps a little algae to round it out. We have discovered, however, that we have better health and live longer if we obtain more variety in minerals and vitamins. We have learned to obtain these directly from the ocean and each house is equipped with its own vitamin plant, with intake pipes leading from the house into the ocean. Unfortunately, the same process which extracts vitamins from sea water also extracts gold. It then has to be separated and thrown out."

"What happens to it then?" Manning asked as they entered the palace.

"Garbage collectors pick it up daily and it is taken to a central fission plant. There, at considerable expense to the royal exchequer, it is transmuted into elements easier to dispose of. I imagine that it's not much different from the garbage problems on other worlds."

"Well—only a little," Manning said dryly.

Moments later he was being ushered into the presence of the emperor of Mizar. The latter looked much like the other Mizarians Manning had seen except that his bill was yellow with age. He sat on a throne which was shaped like a nest.

"We are pleased to see you before us," the emperor said when Manning was announced. He clapped his hands sharply and cried out: "Bring to us the youngest prince of the House of Volat."

A servant came running in, carrying a huge scarlet pillow. In the very center of the pillow there was a solitary egg. It was light blue in color and looked to be about four inches long and perhaps two and a half inches in diameter at the thickest section.

"Look well upon our youngest son," the emperor said to Manning.

Manning looked, but it still looked like any other egg to him. "Very—er—handsome," he said lamely.

"Naturally," the emperor conceded. "This is his Royal Youthful Mostness, the Prince Pyes Razestans Volat. You will recognize him the next time you see him?"

"Of course," Manning lied.

The emperor waved at the servant, and the egg was carried

from the room. "We have requested your presence," the emperor said, "because it has occurred to us that you may not be familiar with all of our customs and we have just appointed you Judge of the Royal Egg Contest. The youngest prince of our house will be entered in that contest and we wished you to understand that your judgment should not be influenced by the fact that he is our son. He should be awarded first prize only if in your detached opinion he is the most beautiful."

"Of course." Manning said.

"That is all," the emperor said in dismissal.

"Just a minute, Your Mostness," Manning said. "I had intended to request an audience this morning and perhaps I can speak to you of a matter which concerns me."

"The audience is granted. Speak."

"I have been concerned," Manning said, "by the amount of anti-Federation and anti-Terran feeling I have seen among your people and by the knowledge that this may still affect your intention of joining the Federation."

"As you can see," the emperor replied, "we share none of this feeling ourselves. We insisted on joining the Federation because we feel the advantages are greater than the disadvantages. There has, however, always been a small political party on Mizar which has been opposed to any sort of relationship with Terra because of your disgusting habit of eating eggs... Recently, we understand that this has been growing."

"Fostered by two other aliens, Dtilla Raishelle of Acrux, and Dzanku Dzanku of Rigel."

"So we understand," the emperor said. "They have not, however, broken any of our laws—we do rather pride ourselves on our free speech. It is also true that if this continues, we must bow to the will of our people and withdraw from the Federation."

"Are you sure that Dzanku Dzanku and Dtilla Raishelle are engaged in no other activity bearing on this?" Manning asked.

"According to our Royal Egg Watchers—what you would call police on your world—they have not."

Manning thought about it a moment. "Can Your Mostness suggest any course of action which might influence the matter in either direction?"

"Your own actions will influence it," the emperor said. "The actions of any Terran would influence it. If you carry off your temporary position well, it may counteract what the others are doing. Should you offend our people or break any of our laws, it would most certainly be the deciding factor in swinging all of our people against joining the Federation. Now, Manning Draco, it distresses us to end this audience, but we believe you are due at a preliminary egg contest and you must be there promptly."

Manning thanked him and left. The equerry was waiting to drive him to the festival and they went there directly. Manning had a slight twinge of conscience about leaving Nisa Brioshe waiting at the hotel, but it was also a relief to get away from her great, staring orange eyes.

A LARGE CROWD of Mizarians was already gathered in the stadium at the Festival. A huge table and reviewing stand had been constructed in the center of it and the table was already covered with pillows of many different colors. On each pillow there was an egg. So far as Manning could see, they all looked exactly alike.

The equerry let Manning out not far from the stadium and drove off. A small group of Mizarians awaited Manning's approach. He was not surprised to notice that among them were Dtilla Raishelle, Dzanku Dzanku, and Sam Warren.

"I am Insta Tuquo," the leader of the delegation said. He introduced the others. "I believe," he added, "that you already know our other three distinguished visitors."

Manning nodded.

"As you may know," Insta Tuquo continued, "each has to have an assistant. In honor of your own origins, we have appointed Mr. Sam Warren as your assistant."

"I can hardly wait," Manning murmured.

Sam Warren grinned. "We'll knock them dead, Manning," he said.

"I wouldn't be surprised if you meant that literally," Manning replied. "I don't know why you want to be my assistant, but just watch your step. Don't try to pull any fast ones."

"Me?" Sam exclaimed with injured innocence.

Manning wasn't fooled. He'd decided that the best he could do was to keep his eyes open and hope he could catch Sam in an anti-Terran conspiracy.

The Mizarians explained that there were still a few entries to arrive and left Manning and Sam on the reviewing stand. A moment later Dzanku strolled over to join them.

"So nice to see you again, Manning," he said. "Where is that luscious little female you brought with you?"

DRACO OPENED his mouth to reply, but his answer was forever lost to posterity, for at that moment one of the Mizarian mothers in the crowd let out a piercing scream. This brought everyone running and for several moments there was so much confusion that it was impossible to find out what had happened. But finally everyone else quieted down enough so that the hysterical mother could be heard.

"Someone," she shrilled, "has taken my baby."

Everyone glanced at the table. Sure enough, one of the pillows was now empty.

Several of the other mothers hastened to comfort the bereaved parent. In the meantime, the official committee, faces grim and bills aquiver, strode to the reviewing stand.

"It is impossible," cried Insta Tuquo, "that a Mizarian would do such a dastardly deed. The aliens must be searched."

It was all happening so quickly that Manning Draco had no time to guess what was going on. Before he could move, a couple of the Mizarians had grabbed him and were searching him. There was a hoarse cry from one of them as he drew a blue egg from Manning's pocket.

"My baby," cried the woman as she recognized it.

"Wait a minute," Manning said, aware of the hostile glances from every direction. "I didn't take that egg. Someone must have put it in my pocket while I was talking to Dzanku—" He broke off and glanced at the Rigelian. "So that was it? You came over to talk to me just to give Sam or Dtilla a chance to grab that egg and put it in my pocket."

"Tut-tut," Dzanku said. "I'm afraid he's really flipped his jets. Everyone knows that Rigelians not only don't eat eggs, but have the utmost respect for them."

"He's right," growled one of the Mizarians. He had Manning firmly by the arm. "Come on, you! We have ways of taking care of eggnappers like you."

CHAPTER SIX

M ANNING DRACO had been in jail for almost a week. Nisa Brioshe had been in to see him twice. The first time he had asked her to get in touch with J. Barnaby Cruikshank and tell him what had happened, but when she returned she told him that she hadn't been permitted to make any calls or send any messages out of Mizar.

Nisa didn't come back after the second visit and the warder told him that he wasn't permitted any more visitors. The guards spoke to him no more than they had to, usually delivering his meals in complete silence. Although he was not served Terran food, he had no complaint other than the monotony of his diet. It consisted exclusively of shellfish and red algae.

He was surprised, therefore, on the morning of the seventh day when the warder came clumping back to the cell shortly after the morning meal.

"Visitor for you," he announced in a surly tone. He unlocked the cell door and led Manning to the visiting room. Manning entered, expecting to find Nisa again, but it was Dtilla Raishelle, the Acruxian, with a glint of triumph in his eyes.

"This," he said, "is the kind of setting in which I like to see you, Manning Draco. How do you like it, my fine simian friend?"

Manning snorted. "Did you just drop around to gloat?"

"Not at all," Dtilla said. "I have the honor of being your attorney."

"What?"

"I have been appointed to defend you on the most serious charge of eggnapping."

"I'm sunk," Manning groaned. "I demand the right to have an attorney from Terra."

"Can't be arranged, old boy."

"But you and Dzanku framed me. Now you're going to be my attorney. The next thing I suppose you'll tell me that Dzanku is going to be the judge."

"Unfortunately, we couldn't arrange that," the Acruxian said gravely.

"What," Manning groaned, "is the penalty for eggnapping?"

The Acruxian was obviously enjoying himself. "The convicted criminal is sentenced to walk out through the water-lock—without any underwater suit."

"How far down are we?"

"About three miles below the surface," Dtilla said. His tentacles waved with pleasure. "I think we've managed the whole thing quite well, don't you?"

"You admit you framed me?" Manning said.

"In the privacy of this room, where no one else can hear me, yes. You'll be interested to know that tomorrow—today is the last day of the Festival—the emperor will announce that Mizar is not joining the Federation. I expect that shortly afterward a treaty will be signed between Mizar and Acrux. We are grateful to you, Manning. Perhaps I can get my government to bestow some honor on you—posthumously, of course."

"Okay," Manning said dryly, "you've had your fun. Scram!"

"Oh, there is one other thing," Dtilla said. "It seems that the

Egg Festival on Mizar is a joyous occasion and it is the custom to be lenient toward crimes committed during the festival. In normal cases, this amounts to a pardon. Your crime, however, was too horrible for anything like that. But there is one way you can be released from prison—today."

Manning knew there was a catch in it or Dtilla wouldn't be telling him about it. "How?" he asked.

"The law states that one accused of a crime committed during the Festival may be released on the last day of the Festival if he challenges his accuser or accusers to mortal combat. It is considered that this combat becomes a test of guilt in the eyes of the gods and if he wins, he is considered innocent. If he loses, then he was obviously properly executed. Officially, I believe, Dzanku and I are both listed as your accusers since Dzanku had earlier predicted that you might try to steal an egg and it was I who suggested to Insta Tuquo that he search you first."

NOW MANNING got it. He had some choice. He could stay in prison and most probably be convicted and executed without a chance of getting in touch with the Federation, or he could go out and fight both Dzanku and Dtilla at the same time. It would make little difference in the long run. Manning had no illusions about it. He had gotten the best of Dzanku Dzanku a number of times, and of Dtilla Raishelle once, but he had been in position to use trickery to some degree. In an open contest, with or without weapons, he would be no match for even one of them. No Terran could match the strength of an Acruxian or a Rigelian, nor could even Manning match them with mental strength.

Still he did not waver in his choice. Once he was outside, there might be something he could turn to his own advantage.

"I'll challenge you," he said.

"Good," Dtilla exclaimed.

With that he turned and left the room.

In less than an hour three guards arrived and took Manning out of the prison. They drove directly to the Festival and they led him into the stadium. It was filled with festive Mizarians. In the middle section, there was a scarlet canopy over the royal box. Evidently the big egg contest had just taken place, for the table with all the eggs on it was still just below the spot where the emperor sat. Manning could see that the winning ribbon was around the egg which rested on the scarlet pillow. Evidently whoever had succeeded Manning as judge had interpreted the emperor's little speech the same way he had.

DTILLA RAISHELLE and Dzanku Dzanku were already out in the center of the stadium. They waited patiently as Manning walked slowly toward them, trying in vain to think of some way out of this. If he could only find some way to throw both of them off guard at the same time, he might do something with mental force. But he knew if he attacked only one, his mind would be vulnerable to the blasting force of the other.

Dtilla Raishelle waved his tentacles as Manning drew near and the excited murmur of the crowd quieted.

"We are pleased to accept your challenge, Manning Draco," he said, "knowing that justice will triumph and that you will prove yourself guilty as charged. Although it is not required by law, Dzanku and myself have come into the stadium unarmed. We do not want to take undue advantage of you."

"Not much," Manning murmured as he stared at them. Each of them weighed at least a ton. Between them they possessed ten tentacles, each one of which was powerful enough to crush a man.

"We have chosen," Dtilla continued, "to leave it simply a contest of strength. Are you ready, Manning Draco?"

"No," Manning said truthfully. "I'd like a little time to limber up my muscles—say about eight or ten years."

"You know," Dzanku said, speaking for the first time, "I rather regret the way this is ending. I've always been rather fond of Manning and he really deserves a better chance. Couldn't we just exile him somewhere?"

"No," snapped Dtilla. "You agreed to take my orders. Such

softness is unworthy of a Rigelian, a cousin of the mighty Acruxians. You know what will happen if I report your softness to Rigel?"

"I know," Dzanku said. "Well, let's get it over with. Sorry, Manning, old friend."

The two of them began a slow, methodical approach toward Manning, their tentacles flicking nervously with the tension. The crowd was hushed and expectant.

Manning's first thought was to run, but he knew it was futile. He'd never raced against an Acruxian or a Rigelian, but he had an idea they could outrun him too. And the hoped-for inspiration still had not come.

Then something happened so swiftly that it was a full minute before Manning realized what it was. He felt a force strike him, even though they were still several yards away; then he had an impression of flying through the air. The next moment he dropped with a thump. It had happened in perhaps ten seconds. It took him the other fifty seconds to realize he was no longer out in the corner of the stadium. He was seated up in the stadium proper. Next to him was Nisa Brioshe.

As his senses returned to him, Manning was aware of the surprised cries from the crowd. Looking down into the field, he realized this action had not been the only startling thing. Dtilla Raishelle and Dzanku Dzanku, their tentacles thrashing madly, were both floating in the air fifteen feet above the ground.

It took a few more seconds to connect what had happened with the girl who sat next to him. He noticed the air of concentration on her face.

"*You* did it?" he asked.

"Yes," she said, without taking her eyes from the two figures out over the field.

"How?"

"Didn't you know?" she asked, sounding surprised. "We of Rasalague are natural teleports. That is why we find it so easy to slip into ships that visit our planet."

"So that's what you had in mind when you offered to help me break out of jail?"

"Yes." She frowned. "But what am I going to do now, Manning? They can't do any harm while I hold them up in the air this way, but I don't know what to do with them."

"Can you handle them separately?" he asked. "I mean can you make one of them do one thing and the other something else?"

"Of course."

"And can you teleport anything else while you're also handling them?"

"I brought you up here at the same time I was picking them up," she said simply.

Manning laughed. He leaned over and whispered in her ear. Then he began climbing down out of the stands.

OUT OVER THE FIELD, Dtilla Raishelle began drifting away across the field while Dzanku Dzanku began to revolve like a pinwheel. He was still revolving when Manning arrived on the field directly beneath him. One of his three eyes managed to catch a glimpse of Manning.

"Manning, old friend," he cried, "make her stop whirling me. It's making me dizzy."

"Will you listen to reason?"

"Yes, yes. Anything if you make her stop. You know I can't stand to be dizzy."

Manning waved one arm and the Rigelian stopped revolving. He stared down out of three bleary eyes.

"Oh, dear," he said. "Dtilla is going to be very angry now. He wanted to get rid of that girl before she started teleporting and I talked him out of it."

"Never mind about Dtilla. I don't think he'll be in a position to do you any great damage. Dzanku, I feel obliged toward you for at least trying to stop Dtilla from killing me, and in addition I have an old score to settle with someone else. Dzanku, if I let you go and give you a tip on how you can make a little money, will you and Sam Warren beat it out of here at once without interfering anymore?"

"Will we!" exclaimed Dzanku.

"Give me your word of honor as a Rigelian gambler?" said Manning, knowing that the only time a Rigelian can be believed is when he swears on his gambling oath.

"I do," Dzanku said with as much dignity as he could muster while hanging fifteen feet in the air.

"Where's Sam?"

"Over by the gate. I telepathed for him to stand by the minute that girl took over."

"All right; I'll have Nisa let you down in a moment. First I want to give you a tip. You know that our old friend J. Barnaby Cruikshank is now Secretary of Planets in the Federation government?"

"I'd heard that he was."

"Well, it's a job that takes all of J. Barnaby's time, so he's left the office in charge of Wellington Shardell, the character who used to be in charge of the Terran territory. Now, I happen to know that he's never told Wellington about you and Sam, and that he destroyed all the records because he doesn't want anyone to know how you fooled him so many times. So I was thinking that good old Wellington might be very happy to get two enterprising insurance salesmen. Get it?"

"Manning, I love you," Dzanku said joyfully. "It's a deal and you have my gambler's word that Sam and I won't be able to get out of here fast enough. This espionage stuff was never in our line anyway. We just took it to tide us over while we looked around."

Manning waved his arm again and Dzanku floated to the ground. He waved to the girl with one tentacle and to Manning with another as he set off across the stadium field. Manning watched and saw Sam Warren join him at the gate. The two of them vanished from sight.

Manning glanced up at Nisa and she nodded. He turned and walked over to stand in front of the royal box. In the meantime, Dtilla Raishelle, his head almost purple with rage, had been floated to the same spot.

"Your Royal Mostness," Manning said, "I beg you to listen to me for a moment."

"We will hear what you have to say, Terran," the emperor said.

"I hope to prove to you," Manning said, "that the unfortunate incident which put me in jail was entirely the work of this Acruxian who has taken advantage of your gracious hospitality. The whole thing was a plot to discredit me as a Terran envoy. While pretending to fight me, Dtilla Raishelle committed the eggnapping which was the real goal of his nefarious scheme!"

As Manning paused, every eye in the stadium looked down to the table that held the eggs—and saw the empty scarlet pillow.

"The Prince," the emperor cried hoarsely.

Due to his rage over his helpless position, Dtilla Raishelle was a little slow to grasp what was going on, but he got it as he heard the emperor's shout. His tentacles hastily fumbled at his pockets and he found the egg in one of them. He drew it out and stared at it a moment. Then his eye-stalks swiveled to focus on Manning.

"You did this!" he shouted in rage. "You and that freak from Rasalague! You—" The tentacle holding the egg drew back as he prepared to hurl it at Manning.

There was an angry shout from the emperor. From a dozen spots Royal Egg Watchers aimed and fired their paralyzers. Every muscle of the raging Acruxian was immediately locked. Manning signaled Nisa and she lowered Dtilla to the ground. Eager hands rescued the royal egg while other hands, no less eager, dragged the Acruxian away.

"We rule that you were unjustly accused," the emperor said to Manning, speaking loudly so that his voice would carry over the entire stadium. "It is clear to us that it is you and the Federation who have always been our friends and that to our shame we were tricked into believing the vile Acruxian. In return for your valiant efforts in saving our Prince Royal, we hereby decree that you, Manning Draco, shall hereafter be recognized as a Royal Egghead of Mizar and accorded all the privileges of our realm, second only to the royal family."

As a roar went up from the crowd, Manning turned and went up into the stands where Nisa was waiting.

"Honey, you were wonderful," he exclaimed, taking her in his arms.

"You were wonderful, too—but that doesn't mean that you're invited to come up to my hotel room."

She looked at him and there was a mischievous glint in her orange eyes. Then she stood up on tiptoe and whispered in Manning's ear.

"Honest?" he said.

She nodded.

Manning threw back his head and laughed. He was still laughing when hundreds of friendly Mizarians descended upon him.

CHAPTER SEVEN

EARLY THE NEXT DAY, Manning Draco and Nisa Brioshe were taken to the surface of Mizar in one of the royal sublimousines. They were soon in the *Alpha Actuary* and blasting skyward. Once they were beyond the atmosphere, Manning threw the ship into magnidrive. Then he motioned to Nisa to stand away from the screen and put in a call to J. Barnaby Cruikshank on Rigil Kentaurus.

"Well, it's all done," he said when J. Barnaby appeared. "Everyone on Mizar dearly loves us and they love me so much that they have made me a Royal Egghead—and if you laugh I'll kill you; it's the highest honor they can give an alien. They're coming into the Federation, on schedule. Dtilla Raishelle has been arrested for committing the most serious crime on Mizar and will probably be executed. Acrux won't be able to complain, considering the nature of his crime— kidnapping the royal prince."

"Dtilla have any accomplices?" J. Barnaby asked.

"None," Manning lied cheerfully. "It's all tied up."

"I knew you'd do it, my boy. I said—"

"The pictures, J. Barnaby," Manning reminded.

"Eh? Oh, yes, the pictures. To be sure, my boy." While Manning watched, J. Barnaby brought out the photographs and the negatives of the pictures that had been taken in Manning's hotel room and destroyed them. "There you are. It was just a joke, my boy. I wouldn't have used them."

"A very funny joke," Manning said. "By the way, how is my old friend Wellington making out running Greater Solarian while you're gone?"

"Quite well," J. Barnaby said. "I understand he's having a little trouble getting good salesmen, but otherwise he's doing fine and I'm sure he'll solve that problem."

"I'm sure he will, too," Manning said. "Give him my love the next time you talk to him. Oh, yes, there's one more thing, J. Barnaby. You mentioned that I might obtain a concession on Mizar."

"As long as it's not something someone here wants," J. Barnaby said cautiously. "What is it you want?"

"I've already arranged to take over all the garbage collections on Mizar. How about putting the official stamp on it?"

"Garbage collections?" J. Barnaby's face peered out of the screen, his expression indicating that he was doubting his son-in-law's sanity. "What do you want with that?"

"Does anybody else want it?"

"I'm sure they don't," J. Barnaby said promptly. "But—"

"Then approve it," Manning said. He turned on a recorder

while. J. Barnaby went through the routine of officially approving Manning Draco's garbage-collecting contract on Mizar.

"But what the blue blazes do you want with garbage?" he demanded again when he had finished. "Isn't there enough garbage on Terra?"

"Oh, I forgot to mention one thing," Manning, said lightly. "The garbage on Mizar consists almost entirely of gold."

He broke the connection while the new expression was still forming on J. Barnaby's face.

IT WAS A FEW hours later when Manning Draco, holding Nisa Brioshe by the hand, arrived home. He strode in through the door and Vega, hearing his footsteps, came running to throw herself into his arms. But just before she reached him, she caught sight of his companion. She stopped short.

"Who's that?" she demanded, "Oh, this is a new friend of mine," he said with a grin. "This is Nisa Brioshe from Rasalague. Nisa, this is my wife, Vega."

"How do you do," Nisa said. "Your husband has been very kind to me."

"I'll bet," Vega said. Her gaze roamed over the other girl. "Especially the way you're dressed. It would naturally play on his sympathy, if you'll excuse the expression."

"Nisa's a great kid," Manning went on. "She stowed away on my ship when I was heading for Mizar, thinking I was coming to Terra. So she just stayed there with me and then I brought her home."

"Manning Draco," Vega said firmly, "tell me truthfully—are you drunk?"

"No."

"Well, I'm going home to my father," she said. "If you think you can brazenly bring that—that—" She was staring in amazement at Nisa. "What's wrong with her?"

Manning looked and saw that Nisa was shaking violently as though in the grip of a terrible chill. Her hands were clawing at the scarf around her neck and her face was contorted with a sort of ecstatic pain.

"This is why I brought her home," Manning said softly. "Wait."

Nisa Brioshe stripped the scarves from her throat and from her body. As they fell around her feet, leaving her completely nude, a red line was visible down the center of her body.

As they watched, the line grew even redder. The flesh on her body and her face seemed to be moving with a life of its own. Then, suddenly, she split in two. The complete crack started in the exact center of her face and ran swiftly down her body. And even as it happened, her flesh writhed and flowed—and each leg became two, a new arm appeared on each half, other organs swiftly grew and rounded out. And standing before them were two small, nude figures. One of them was quite obviously male, the other still female.

The both smiled shyly at the Dracos, then, clasping hands, turned and ran from the house.

"That's the real reason I brought her home," Manning said. "Her fission was about to take place and I didn't want her to have to experience it out on the street. Although I'll also admit that I thought you might hear about her being with me and I wanted you to see why she wouldn't be interested in me."

(Nisa Brioshe had herself told Manning the secret of Rasalaguan mating. When the Rasalaguan is ready for mating, she leaves her own planet and goes to another world. The reason for this is purely psychological, giving the Rasalaguan a pleasant honeymoon to make up for its brevity. Sometime shortly after arriving there she divides by fission into a male and a female. As soon as the male has impregnated the female, he dies. The female then returns home to bear her children, all of whom will be female.)

"But I don't understand," Vega said. She looked at the scarves on the floor, then stared out in the direction the couple had vanished. "Where were they running to?"

Manning grinned. "I'll explain it to you step by step," he said, "starting with a kiss." He held his arms out and Vega ran into them. She didn't seem to mind in the least that the explanation stopped being vocal at that point.

ACT THREE / 3470

THE AGILE ALGOLIAN

Author's note: There have been so many letters (well, at least one) asking how Manning Draco got started and how he developed a secondary mind shield (the only one among the Terrans) that I have decided to take you back in time—back to the year 3470, when Manning Draco was unaware that he had any abilities other than the talents of an ordinary insurance investigator and a first-class ogler of shapely girls.   —K.F.C.

CHAPTER ONE

MANNING DRACO had been out of the hospital for the better part of two weeks, but the Medical Monopoly had kept him hanging around on Rigil Kentaurus while the pharmaceutical pundits scratched their heads and muttered the mystical phrases of their profession. If it hadn't been for a generous supply of nurses, who were interested in a quite different branch of research, Manning might well have fused his jets in frustration.

Six months had passed since the accident. That night he had just finished the case of the Dented Denebian and was relaxing in the Twilight Zone of Sin City on Hamal. He had made the mistake of getting into an argument with a six-armed Kochabian and had been thoroughly and scientifically trounced. He had come to a week later in the hospital. Diagnosis: various severe bruises, six broken ribs, one broken leg, and concussion.

He had, however, healed nicely and a month before his release had progressed to the point where he could chase, and catch, the fleetest nurses. His release was only a formality until he came to the cybernetic mind-reading required of all head-injury patients before they were permitted to return to work. He had gone through many a cybernetic M-R, but this time something went wrong. The machine blew a fuse. When it was repaired, they tried again. The reading revealed that there was only one thought in Manning Draco's head, a performance considerably below par for the average moron. And that one thought caused the doctors—all elderly gentlemen who had long ago given up fleshly pursuits—to blush.

The findings of the machine, which had not been wrong in

five centuries, might have given pause to a more serious-mind-ed young man, but Manning took it in his stride. He was quite willing to admit that he had only one thought at the moment and wanted no more. He was even annoyed at the doctors who kept pulling him away from that one thought in order to try to find out why he was so single-minded.

They had about decided that in some freak way a large slice of skull bone had been driven into his brain, shielding a large portion of it, when the whole matter was taken out of their hands. Otherwise they might have gone on carving up Manning until there was nothing left to withstand their skill.

The interference came, as it always does in such cases, from

above. Prior to his accident, Manning Draco had been chief investigator for the Greater Solarian Insurance Company, Monopolated, presided over by J. Barnaby Cruikshank. In absence of any proof that the accident had occurred on his own time, he had remained on salary while in the hospital. All of this had been well enough while the regular investigators had been able to handle the cases that came up. But then there came a case, cutting painfully into J. Barnaby's bank account, which he knew was beyond their abilities. The President of Greater Solarian set up a shout for his chief investigator.

It was practically impossible to ignore adverse reports from a cybernetic M-R, but to J. Barnaby Cruikshank the impossible was simply an impudent affront. He put in a visicall to the President of the Federation and quickly reduced that gentleman to the psychological state of an office boy. When he finally broke the connection, the president merely passed along the same treatment to his Secretary of Internal Affairs. And so the hot, angry words of J. Barnaby were passed down along the line until finally an underling screamed the insults at the chief doctor of the Rigil Kentaurus Hospital.

Ten minutes later Manning Draco was discharged and the offending cybernetic report had vanished from the records.

WITHIN A MATTER of two hours, Manning strode cheerfully into the main offices of Greater Solarian in Nyork. He grinned down at the receptionist, but her answering expression was one of relief rather than the welcome he'd expected.

"Go on in," she said wearily. "He's been calling me every five minutes to ask if you've arrived."

"Tell him to simmer down," Manning said and passed on through the offices.

Outside the private office of the president, he hesitated until the door-scanner recognized him and the door swung open. He stepped inside and faced his employer.

At a mere thirty-eight, J. Barnaby Cruikshank had been the president and chief stockholder of a company that held a galactic-wide monopoly. It was true that he had inherited the company, but until his accession it had been a small outfit, insuring only humans. Under J. Barnaby, Greater Solarian had started issuing policies to cover every form of life in the galaxy. It had prospered and J. Barnaby was one of the richest and most influential men in the Federation.

J. Barnaby was a man of great urbanity, but it had already worn thin at the edges. His hair was mussed and his plastic sport coat ("Guaranteed not to wrinkle") was wrinkled.

"It's about time," he growled at the sight of his employee. "What did you do—walk back?"

Manning grinned as he dropped into a chair. "Some welcome," he said.

"Welcome!" said J. Barnaby, looking at the ceiling for moral support. "You've just had a six-month vacation at my expense in the finest hospital."

"With hot and cold running nurses," added Manning. "But don't forget I was grievously wounded while conducting certain investigations." He carefully neglected to make it clear that the inquiry had been into the morals of a Ganymedean dancing girl rather than an insurance problem.

"I have my suspicions about that," J. Barnaby said darkly. With what must have been an inner struggle, he smoothed the anger from his face and replaced it with what he fondly imagined was a friendly smile. "Of course, we're glad to have you back, Manning, my boy. The thoughts of all of us here at Greater Solarian were with you during your months of pain and—"

"Don't overdo it," Manning said. "A little bit of your sympathy goes a long way. Now, what's the crisis?"

"Well, there is a small matter," J. Barnaby admitted. He paused, as if in doubt. "You sure you feel up to a little work?"

"If I didn't, you'd prop me up on crutches and send me out anyway. What is it?"

CRUIKSHANK DROPPED his interest in Manning's health with alacrity.

"Well," he said, "during the past year we've been taking quite a beating on joint life policies. There have been seventy-two thousand, one hundred and ten cases of husbands and wives taking out joint policies and then of one of the couple dying within a matter of days."

"The dangers of matrimony," Manning said. "All of the policies sold by the same man?"

"The same two. Sam Warren and Jaba Woo, an Algolian. They've been working together for some time and both have excellent records. I'd hate to think they were involved."

"Any other suspects?"

"A few," J. Barnaby said. "All of the cases have taken place within a radius of two light-years of Canopus. Warren and Woo have their headquarters on Canopus I. Unfortunately, the similarity between all these cases did not come to our attention until about a month ago. We've done some preliminary check-ing. In each case, the official records show that the deceased husband or wife died from natural or accidental causes, but in no case was there an autopsy. And in each case, there was a quick funeral, all handled by the same undertaker."

Manning looked his question.

"A Canopusian outfit," said J. Barnaby, "called the Happy Asteroid Mortuary. It's run by someone named Encycla Grave. He's probably an Algolian."

"*Asteroid* Mortuary?"

"Yeah," J. Barnaby grunted. "He specializes in fancy funerals. Each one of the insured was buried on a small asteroid which was then power-driven into space. That's why we haven't been able to get an autopsy on a single one of them. Incidentally, in each case, the cost of the funeral was exactly one-half the amount of the insurance policy."

"Clever," Manning said. "Is that all you've got on him?"

"Not quite. We've had one bit of luck. Last week the patrol was over near Betelgeuse searching for smugglers. They stopped to investigate a stray asteroid. It was one of the asteroid crypts.

When they saw what was on it, they threw a magnetic plate on it and brought it in. I got the report yesterday. A Mrs. Henry Orbson, Terran, was buried on it. She died about six months ago while she and her husband were spending their vacation on Canopus. A week before she died, she and her husband had taken out joint policies. Her husband collected two hundred thousand credits from us. The death certificate had stated that Mrs. Orbson died from a heart attack. Well, the heart attack was brought on by a sharp knife being drawn across her throat."

"Who signed the death certificate?"

"Encycla Grave," J. Barnaby said sourly. "He belongs to the Medical Monopoly as well as being a mortician."

"A nice racket," Manning said. "How come you haven't had him arrested?"

"There's more to it than this," said J. Barnaby. "As I said, the funerals are quick. The lady was buried in the dress she was wearing, and in the pocket of it there was a letter—addressed to her husband. Here it is." He fished among the papers on his desk and came up with a letter. He handed it to Manning.

THE MARITAL RELATIONS BUREAU
27 Circle Square (Upper)
City of Sentiment
Canopus (I)

March 42, 3470
(Solarian date)

Mr. Henry Orbson
Galactic Rest Hotel
City of Sentiment
Dear Sir:

At first guess, you might say that you have no marital problems. But are you happy? Or have you reached a time when the vows that bind you "until death do us part" are beginning to chafe? Does your wife nag and scold? Has she lost her beauty? Is there a younger woman in your future?

These are all questions which the man of intelligence must ask himself from time to time. If you are able to answer most of them in the negative, then you are a fortunate man and I congratulate you. If the answers are yes, I can do better than congratulate you. I can set you free.

There is *no charge* for a consultation. (In fact, you may *make a profit* out of the matter.) I guarantee satisfaction and there is no charge until after I have succeeded in eliminating the obstacle to your happiness. Even then the fee is modest.

Why not see me at your convenience?

Sincerely yours,
Nottyl Nadyl

"Who is this Nadyl?" Manning asked when he'd finished reading the letter.

"Another Algolian,[21] I think," J. Barnaby said. "You see how the letter implies that Nadyl will get rid of the guy's wife, without being evidence against him? There's no proof that Orbson went to see Nadyl, but two days after the date of this letter he bought the insurance policies. And one week later his wife died. And she was murdered."

"I gather that you think there's an Algolian in the money pile," Manning said dryly. "Or, rather, three of them. An Algolian undertaker, an Algolian heart-throb character, an Algolian insurance salesman, and Sam Warren. Is that all of them?"

"I don't think so. All the asteroid crypts were bought from the same place. There's a Rigelian named Dzanku Dzanku—calls himself Dizzy Dzanku, the Honest Rigelian—who's a second-hand asteroid dealer. He bought up several hundred used asteroids from the Mining Monopoly and has them in a close-formation orbit around Canopus, about five hundred miles from the surface. He does a fair vacation rental business, but he also supplies them to this Nadyl character."

---

21   At that time, very little was known about Algolians. There were several of them doing business throughout the galaxy, but under the treaty of 3106, Terrans were forbidden to visit Algol for any purpose. All the Algolians who had been seen were completely different from one another in appearance and it was assumed that there were dozens, if not hundreds, of different species of Algol, all of them intelligent. Consequently, it was difficult to be sure who was an Algolian unless you were able to see his identity papers.

"You got anything tying him in with the scheme?" Manning asked.

"No," J. Barnaby grunted. "But if he's an honest Rigelian, then he's the only one in the universe. You know that Rigel has a criminal culture, so you can bet if there's something crooked going on, this Dizzy Dzanku's in on it."

"Okay," Manning said. He stood up. "I'll go take a look."

"Not so fast," J. Barnaby said. "I've got the whole thing planned out. The way it is, we could have this Henry Orbson and the undertaker arrested and make it stick. But that wouldn't break up the whole ring. We're going to set a trap for them."

MANNING SCOWLED. "We?" he asked with heavy irony. "Whenever you start talking about what *we* are going to do, *I* get a cold wind on the back of my neck."

"Nonsense, my boy," J. Barnaby said briskly. "I have every confidence in you. Now, here's the setup. Instead of going there as Manning Draco, insurance investigator, you'll—what is your middle name again?"

"Melvin," Manning said reluctantly.

"Splendid. You're going to Canopus as Melvin Draco, a tired young businessman on vacation. Rent one of the asteroids so you'll be away from it all. I've arranged for someone to go along and pose as your wife and all you have to do is wait until—"

"Wait a minute," Manning said. "If your idea is to send some old hag along with me and then expect me to wait around while she hires some guy to cut my throat, you can get yourself another boy."

The visiscreen industry lost a great actor when J. Barnaby Cruikshank became a magnate. He could whip up a few tears and a reproachful expression at the drop of an accusation. "You wrong me, my dear boy," he said sadly. "I wouldn't think of putting your life in jeopardy. As I was about to say, it will appear that your wife is a nag and that you are heartily sick of her. Then all you do is wait to be contacted—probably by this marital relations individual—and make a deal for him to kill your wife after you've taken out insurance on her life. How does that sound?"

"Two objections. First, I still don't like the idea of being cooped up with some old crow you picked out. Second—what if something slips up and she is killed?"

"We will take up the old crow aspect in a moment," said J. Barnaby. "As to the second objection, she is an Aliothan. They are rather difficult to kill by ordinary methods. I trust that the matter will be concluded before the assassin discovers she is from Alioth."

Manning tried to conjure up a picture of an Aliothan, but he couldn't remember ever having seen one. "What do Aliothans look like?" he asked suspiciously.

"Completely humanoid in appearance," J. Barnaby said cheerfully. "Also in most of their habits, I might add. You are ready to leave at once?"

"I suppose so," Manning said reluctantly.

"Good." J. Barnaby leaned forward and touched a key on the interoffice plate of his visiphone. "You may now send in Miss Sera," he said.

Manning Draco waited with some trepidation. He was well aware of J. Barnaby's attitude concerning his interest in comely wenches and he could hardly imagine that this was anything but some female who would give him nightmares for months to come. In a way, he was right.

The door to the office opened.

"Manning," J. Barnaby said, "this is Fanya Sera—to be known hereafter as Mrs. Melvin Draco. Miss Sera, this is Manning Draco."

"How do you do," Fanya said demurely.

FOR SEVERAL seconds, Manning could only gape. What stood in the doorway was nothing short of a vision. She looked exactly like a Terran woman—but one such as he had seldom seen. She was tall, only two or three inches shorter than he, and every inch of her was a dream in curving flesh. So far as he could see—and her dress did little to limit sight—everything that should have been there was there to the fullest degree and nothing was missing. Her hair was long and golden blond. Her eyes were gray-blue, her lips a soft red, her features flawless.

"Hello," Manning finally managed weakly.

"I believe," J. Barnaby said with malice, "we were having some discussion about old crows…"

"That," Manning said quickly, "was merely the crow I intended eating… does Miss Sera know about our assignment?"

"She does."

"Far be it from me to discourage any part of this," Manning said, "but do you think anyone is going to look at her and believe that I want to get rid of her?"

"I think they will," J. Barnaby said. "Miss Sera, you might show Mr. Draco one of your lesser talents."

The girl nodded and there was a glint of humor in her eyes. "Melvin Draco," she said, "if you think you're going to drag me all the way out here and then just keep me cooped up on a silly old asteroid—well, I'm not going to stand for it!" Her voice had suddenly taken on a whine so jarring that Manning found himself wishing she were dead.

"Turn it off," he said shuddering. "And promise me you'll use it only when necessary."

"I promise," she said. Her voice was soft and seductive again and she was smiling invitingly.

"You're right, J. Barnaby," Manning said. "When do we leave?"

"Right now. I've left orders for the cashier to give you enough money to cover expenses. Good luck, my boy."

"How can I miss?" Manning muttered, giving the blonde a meaningful glance as he held the door open for her.

CHAPTER TWO

I T WAS LESS than an hour later when Manning Draco's ship, the *Alpha Actuary*, blasted off from the main Nyork spaceport. As soon as he was clear of Terra's atmosphere, he fed the position of Canopus I into the automatic pilot and gave up the controls. It was 650 light years to Canopus—just far enough to be a pretty dull trip ordinarily, but Manning didn't expect it to be this time.

It could never be said that he was one to waste valuable time. He had barely put the ship on automatic control when he was showing the blonde the special features on the *Alpha Actuary*. She seemed to be properly impressed by the miniature computer, the audio-reader, the demagnetizer, the geoscope, the impulse-translator, and the robosmith. Manning used the latter to make her a pair of gold earrings.

"Thank you, Manning," she said. She gave him a half-veiled glance that seemed all promise. "I never knew Terrans were so nice."

"This is only the beginning, baby," Manning said. "Since we're soon going to start fooling the natives into thinking we're man and wife, don't you think we might get in a little practice first? You could start by showing your gratitude in a more tangible form."

She laughed, a soft musical sound that made Manning's skin feel prickly. It hardly sounded as if he were being repulsed, so he stepped toward her.

He reached out with his arms and at the same time bent to meet her lips. It seemed to him that she swayed to meet him. Then, just before he touched her, something struck him; it jarred his whole body and tore at his nerves until they were ragged. He staggered away and the jarring stopped. His teeth still hurt, however, until he realized that his jaws were clenched.

"What in space was that?" he demanded.

The blonde smiled, but there was something close to disappointment in her eyes. It encouraged Manning to try again.

Once again he got within an inch of her, so close that he could feel the warmth from her skin and his senses were drunk with her perfume, before the giant invisible hand picked him up and shook him until his teeth rattled. It took all of his strength to pull away, but he succeeded just before he was about to black out. His head ached as he backed away.

"What—what happened?" he asked as soon as he could.

This time the blonde laughed. "I'm sorry," she said, and she seemed to be despite the laughter, "but you'll have to ask Mr. Cruikshank."

"J. Barnaby? What's he got to do with it?"

"I promised I wouldn't tell you." She hesitated, then went on: "Manning, I'm truly sorry—but it won't last forever."

For once in his life, Manning Draco was not to be consoled by the promise in a woman's eyes and voice. He retreated to the other end of the ship and sulked.

LATER, WHEN FANYA Sera went into the small stateroom to sleep, an angry Manning Draco put in a visicall to Terra. He was even oblivious of the fact that it was probably well after J. Barnaby's bedtime. A sleepy butler tried to convince him that the hour was untimely, but failed. A few minutes later J. Barnaby, rubbing the sleep from his eyes, appeared on the screen.

"What are you up to?" Manning demanded.

If there had been any doubt that J. Barnaby Cruikshank was up to something, his appearance would have removed it. Normally, any interference with the slumber of the president of Greater Solarian would have resulted in an explosion of temper like a major planet-quake. Instead, however, he was staring out of the screen with the benign expression of an indulgent uncle.

"My dear boy," he said sweetly, "what are you talking about?"

"You know damn well what I'm talking about," Manning snapped. "This Fanya Sera. What did you do to her?"

"I am a happily married man," J. Barnaby said solemnly. "It never occurred to me to do anything to her."

"You know what I'm talking about. Every time I get within an inch of her, something starts shaking my teeth loose."

"Oh, that." J. Barnaby managed the impossible feat of a chuckle that was both fatherly and sinister. "As a matter of fact, she is equipped with a little device I insisted upon. If you were the father of a growing girl, as I am, you'd probably be more familiar with it. Known as the Parents' Comforter, it uses ultrasonic sound to fend off predatory males. I suppose you might call it an ultrasonic chastity belt. But you'll be perfectly safe as long as you keep your passes visual." The chuckle grew into a full-blown laugh.

"Very funny," snarled the man. "Why?"

"You might say I had three reasons, my boy. I wanted to be sure that you kept your mind on the business at hand, something I knew would be difficult once you caught sight of Miss Sera. Then you are supposed to give the picture of a man who wants to get rid of his wife, and the Canopusians are famous for the habit of peeking through keyholes."

"And the third reason?" Manning prompted.

"Believe me, my boy, I also did it for your own protection," J. Barnaby said in his most fatherly manner. "I have an abiding concern for your welfare."

Manning told J. Barnaby what he could do with his paternal concern. Although humanity had progressed far by the 35th century, there had been very little improvement in such suggestions and his words were almost the same as might have been spoken two thousand years earlier. The censor on Procyon covered her ears tightly. If one of the men hadn't been an important figure in the Federation, she would have jammed the call. As it was, she merely tried not to listen and hoped that no one else was tapping that frequency.

J. Barnaby laughed as he broke the connection. The ship's screen faded to a dull gray, leaving Manning more frustrated than before.

Sitting in the comfortable pilot-chair, Manning finally caught a few hours' sleep, but it was far from restful and he awakened in pretty much the same mood.

When Fanya Sera rejoined him, he tried to maintain a dignified silence. But it was almost impossible to sulk in the presence of so much beauty. Finally, he got the idea of trying to talk her into removing the ultrasonic device—whatever it was. It was a lost cause. She was flattered by his eagerness, but that was all.

"I promised Mr. Cruikshank I wouldn't remove it until we were finished with the case," she said. She gave him a lingering glance. "I didn't promise anything about what would happen when you've cleaned it up."

"Is that the best we can do?" Manning asked.

She smiled. "What's wrong, honey?" she asked. "Afraid it'll take you a long time to solve this?"

He gave her a hard look. "Baby," he said, "you're going to see speed that will make your head spin."

WITHIN AN HOUR, they were entering the atmosphere of Canopus I. With the ship back on manual, Manning brought it down on instructions from the spacetower.

They stepped out of the ship to find it surrounded by Canopusians, eyes staring avidly and hearing-hairs quivering with eagerness.[22] Those nearest reached out with their tentacles and lightly touched the cloth of Manning's coat. There was something amusing about their boundless curiosity, although he also knew it could become tiresome. Terrans, visiting Canopus for the first

---

22   The origin of Canopusians is unknown and they seem to be unrelated to any other life form in the galaxy. Their bodies and heads are all of one piece, looking somewhat like inverted gourds. A Canopusian has two short, stubby legs. His tentacles, two of them, are located about midway on his body. On the head-part, there is a tiny, bud-like mouth. He has two eyes, similar in shape to those of humans, and a third one which is on the end of a thin, three-inch eye-stalk. This eye-stalk is flexible and is primarily used for peering around corners and into rooms—to most Terrans it is known as their "keyhole peeper." On the top of his head, the Canopusian has two circular rows of stiff hair. The outer row consists of hearing-hairs and the inner ones are olfactory in nature. The Canopusian is about three feet tall and his smooth flesh is pale lemon in color.

time, could never get used to being followed by a crowd of Canopusians.

"Melvin," said Fanya, "why are those horrible little creatures staring at us?" She was using the special voice again and Manning shuddered.

"I don't know, my dear," he said, trying to keep in character. "But I'll—" He stopped and gaped. At the sound of Fanya's voice, the Canopusians' hearing-hairs had all started agitating violently. Then they turned and scampered away across the spaceport. It was the first time Manning had ever known them to act in such a manner, but he didn't blame them.

After going through spaceport customs, Manning and Fanya got an aircab and directed the driver to take them to the Terran Place Hotel. A few minutes later they were flying over Canopusia, capital of the planet and one of the largest cities in the galaxy.

Canopusia was one of the wonders of the modern universe. Tourists came from all over the Federation merely to see the city about which they had heard so much. It had been described by one visiscreen commentator as a monument to the mentality of the natives. Canopusians, as has been noted, were inquisitive and incurable gossips; further, they had no recognizable system of logic. This was well illustrated by their major city. Streets ran in every which way, a single street sometimes crossing itself seven or eight times. The name of a street would often change in the middle of a block. Other races who had spent a lifetime there still couldn't find their way around the city. (The Canopusians couldn't either, but they didn't care.) As a result the largest single profession on the planet was that of guide.

Almost the entire city had been built before other races had descended on Canopus, and the buildings showed the same lack of concern. There were skyscrapers running up seventy and eighty stories in which there were no elevators or in which floors were constructed in such haphazard split-level design that you couldn't find a particular floor without a guide. Many buildings, residential and professional, stood empty because the builders had neglected to include any sort of entrance. All of this had produced two schools of thought: one convinced that Canopusians were pretty stupid and the other contending that they just didn't give a damn.

Canopusia was a thriving city, but almost all industry and commerce was carried on by other races. Similarly, the guides were all foreigners, although limited to those races with phenomenal memories.

ARRIVING AT THE HOTEL, Manning registered and they were escorted to a suite by a Canopusian bellboy, accompanied by an official guide. He could hardly wait until they were inside and the bellboy and guide were gone, for Fanya had never stopped yakking at him in that shrill voice from the time they had left the spaceport. The shrewish whine finally trailed off as the door closed, leaving them alone. "How am I doing?" she asked in her normal voice.

It was such a relief that Manning, without thinking, swung a gentle slap at a rounded and attractive portion of her anatomy. It was a mistake, for he in turn was slapped silly by ultrasonic waves.

He recovered, cursing J. Barnaby with heartfelt emotion. As he did so, he saw a Canopusian third eye retreating through the keyhole. He laughed in spite of himself.

"As much as I hate to admit it," he said. "J. Barnaby did have a good idea. Canopusians being what they are, it won't be an hour before the entire city knows that Mrs. Draco wears some sort of contraption which clobbers her husband every time he tries to touch her and that Mrs. Draco also has a voice that sounds like an atomic saw trying to chew through asteroid ore, and never stops using it. That ought to bring the wife-killer on the run." He glanced at the blonde and couldn't see how anything so softly rounded could be practically indestructible. "Baby," he said, "are you sure that this isn't going to be dangerous for you?"

"Positive," she said. "But it's nice of you to worry." She blew him a kiss—which was about as satisfactory as such things always are. "What do we do now?"

"I shall admire you for a moment—from a distance," he added hastily. "It'll give time for the word to spread. Then I think I'll go see this second-hand asteroid dealer. Leaving you at home, I might add. There's going to be a limit to how much I can take of your public manners until this is over. Want me to call room service and have something to eat sent up?"

She shook her head. "I don't need anything. My metabolism is quite different from yours."

"Meaning you don't eat?"

"Not as often as you Terrans, at least," she said. "I may be hungry in a few days—it all depends..." Her voice trailed off without revealing on what it depended. But as he stared at the sensuous curves of her body, there was probably nothing which interested Manning less than her eating habits.

"That reminds me," he said. "Where have you been all my life? I've been around, but I don't think I ever saw an Aliothan before."

She had seated herself at the built-in vanity table and was combing her hair. It gleamed in the light like gold threads. "Probably not," she said. "Very few of us have ever been off our planet. This is my own first trip and it was only possible because Mr. Cruikshank arranged it."

"Why?"

She hesitated, then faced him with a funny little smile. "It's a kind of inequality of sexes," she said. "It's only the women of Alioth who are not allowed to leave the planet."

"All the men travel about in the galaxy?"

"Well—all the single men." She stood up and stretched seductively, her breasts straining against the wisp of silk. "But when an Aliothan man marries, he never leaves his wife."

"That I can understand" Manning said fervently. "I can appreciate Aliothan men not wanting the competition they'd have if the rest of the universe knew about you. Have they always penned you in like that?"

She shrugged. "As long as I can remember we've been restricted to Alioth—except when special permission is granted in a case such as this."

"They can't do this to you," Manning said hotly. "Does the Federation know about this?"

"They know about it."

"I'll speak to J. Barnaby about it when we get back," Manning promised. He started to reach out to pat her on the shoulder, but quickly thought better of it. "He's a big man and he can do something if he wants to. I'll tell him he either sees that you're permitted to go where you want to, or I'll go back to Alioth with you."

"I'd like that," she said softly.

Her voice was so provocative that Manning was about to renew his plea for the removal of the ultrasonic device when there was a knock on the door. Muttering his opinion of visitors in general, he went to see who it was.

THE FIGURE who stood in front of the door was enough to make a man slam the door quick. He (she? it?) was as tall as Manning, but there the resemblance ended. His body was rectangular, covered with bits of gayly colored cloth, and supported on three sturdy legs. His head was a perfect square, with one eye and a mouth opening on each of four sides. In the center of the top of his head there was a growth of stiff, antennae-like hair. A ribbon was tied about it some four inches above his head, and the remaining five inches of hair flopped out over it so that it gave the appearance of a mushroom.

"We don't want any," Manning said. He started to close the door.

"Please," said the figure, holding up a broad, flat tentacle. He hissed his sibilants, a common practice among many of the galactic races when they spoke Terran. "I would introduce myself."

"Go ahead," Manning said ungraciously.

"I am Angus McBlla, in all modesty the best guide on

Canopus." The eye facing Manning winked slowly. "I am what you might call a black market guide. I will give you service for twenty percent less than any other guide and with fifty percent more efficiency. I am sufficiently bonded to cover all accidents which may befall you."

"That's nice," Manning said drily. He was about to add that he hardly needed a guide to find his way around in his room, when he decided he might as well get the next step of his case over. "Just a minute," he said. He turned back to the blonde. "There's a guide here, dear. I might as well go find out about renting one of those asteroids."

"All right," she called. She was using the shrew-voice again. "But you hurry right back here, Melvin Draco. I didn't travel six hundred and fifty light years just to sit in a hotel room—"

"Yes, dear," Manning said, closing the door gently but firmly. He walked down the corridor with the guide.

"The lady has—ah—a well-developed voice," Angus McBlla said carefully. His shock of hair seemed to be still quivering.

Manning was about to point out that everything about the lady was well-developed when he realized that was hardly the role for a man who wanted to get rid of his wife. "You can say that again, brother," he said.

"Did you wish to go somewhere?" the guide inquired politely. "Or did you merely wish to get out of the room?"

Manning laughed. "I can see you've had experience with Terrans," he said. "I want to find a second-hand asteroid dealer named Dzanku Dzanku. Know where he's located?"

"The *honest* Rigelian? It is well that you asked me to guide you. His place is in the center of town and most difficult to find. But Angus McBlla will take you there with ease. Come."

CHAPTER THREE

THE RIGELIAN'S place of business occupied a corner lot in the center of Canopusia. Across two sides of the lot there were huge banners announcing his presence:

"DIZZY" DZANKU, THE HONEST RIGELIAN— KING OF THE SECOND-HAND ASTEROIDS—MY PRICES ARE SO LOW YOU'RE CRAZY IF YOU DON'T TAKE ADVANTAGE OF ME.

A small one-room bungalow snuggled in one corner of the lot. There were, of course, no actual asteroids on the lot, but it was filled with scaled models of the ones he had to rent or sell.

Angus McBlla accompanied Manning to the corner and then went into a sense-lounge[23] to wait until he had concluded his business. Manning entered the office of the Honest Rigelian.

The individual in the office was undoubtedly a Rigelian. He was no taller than Manning, but he probably weighed at least a ton by Terra standards. His thick, square torso was supported by two legs, each as thick as a tree trunk. From the upper part of his body projected six tentacles. His face was small and expressionless, with three eye-stalks raised several inches above it.

For a moment the Terran and the Rigelian stared at each other. As J. Barnaby had pointed out earlier, if this were an honest Rigelian, then it would probably be the only one that Manning would ever see. Yet in some mysterious fashion he had the distinct impression that this one was honest. Since he had come expecting to believe just the opposite, this was surprising. In the meantime, he noticed that the Rigelian was regarding him with something like astonishment in each of his three eyes.

---

23   Due to the Anti-Sense League and the McCarrion Space Entry Act of 3159, sense-lounges are unknown on Terra, but they are found in great numbers on most other planets which have considerable intergalactic traffic. They are primarily for those races with more complex and sensitive sense organs and humans can stay in them any length of time without having any reaction at all. A sense-lounge will have numerous small cubicles into which patrons can retire. The cubicle is then filled with a combination of sounds and smells which are intoxicating.

"You are a Terran?" the Rigelian finally asked.

"Of course," Manning said.

"Strange… you must be a new model. I can't ever remember meeting one quite like you.…"

"What's so strange about me?" Manning demanded.

The Rigelian realized that he was hardly acting in the proper way to a potential customer and his tentacles waved in mild agitation. "I—that is—you seem somewhat more distinctive than the average Terran," he said. It was obvious that he was lying, an interesting fact in itself since Rigelians were noted for their smooth lying. "Can I help you in some way?"

"I'm looking for Mr. Dzanku."

"You've found him," the Rigelian said, recovering his professional enthusiasm. "I am Dizzy Dzanku, the Honest Rigelian. Every asteroid comes with a ninety-day guarantee. If it's a crypt-asteroid you're interested in, I guarantee those for life." He gave a well rehearsed laugh.

"My name is Melvin Draco," Manning said. "The little woman and I are up here on a vacation and I want to rent an asteroid."

"I see," Dzanku said, rubbing his tentacles together. "I have some rather fine Honeymoon Specials.…"

"No honeymoon," Manning said sourly. He hoped that he sounded like a jaded husband. "But I would like something fairly quiet so my wife can't be inviting too many people to drop in on us. I'm up here for a rest."

"Of course," the Rigelian said. He glanced shrewdly at Manning. "Something with twin bedrooms, perhaps?"

"Fine," Manning said. "If they are also soundproofed, so much the better."

"To be sure," said Dzanku, with an air of having dealt with such Terrans before. "I have several which I think might fill the bill. Would you like to step out to look at the models?"

They went out on the lot where the Rigelian displayed his models. There were several asteroids that seemed about right. Those that were for rent had small modern homes, equipped with the latest model of robot-servants, and included a small spaceabout for trips down to the planet. Manning finally settled on one which was also furnished with a tiny hunting lodge at a good safe distance from the main house. He paid the advance rent and the Rigelian assured him that the spaceabout would be at the port by the time he could arrive there.

Manning stopped at the sense-lounge for the guide, who seemed a trifle gayer for his pick-me-up, and they returned to the hotel. He checked out and Angus McBlla guided him and Fanya back to the spaceport. He insisted on giving Manning his visinumber in case his services might be needed later. Then Manning and Fanya blasted off for the asteroid.

The next two days passed pleasantly enough—except for the fact that Manning Draco still had to keep his distance with one of the most beautiful blondes he had ever seen. The efficiency of the device she wore was enough to make a man lose faith in modern science.

ON THE MORNING of the third day, a Canopusian copter dropped by the asteroid and left some mail, one letter addressed to Mr. Melvin Draco. It was from the Marital Relations Bureau of Canopus and its contents were almost identical with the letter Manning had seen in the Greater Solarian office.

"Well, it looks like we're getting somewhere, baby," he told Fanya. "It won't be long now."

Her blue eyes were intense as she stared back at him. "It can't be too soon for me," she said.

Manning was flattered that her eagerness seemed to match his own. He had noticed her becoming more tense and restless during the two days they had been on the asteroid.

"There's just one thing I don't understand," he said. "How did J. Barnaby manage to instill such loyalty in you? Why bother to keep your word, since he is so obviously using you?"

"It's not loyalty," she answered. "The device I'm wearing broadcasts a signal to a receiver in Mr. Cruikshank's office. If I remove it, he will know it at once and he swore he could have the space patrol here before I—before we would even have a chance to get acquainted."

"He would, too," Manning said, adding a few choice observations on the man who was his superior.

"But," she said softly, "he promised that he would disconnect the receiver the minute he heard from you that the case is solved."

"There must be a catch in it somewhere," grumbled Manning. "I never knew J. Barnaby to be so generous. But, in the meantime, I'd better run along and see our Mr. Nadyl."

She blew him a kiss as he left the house.

On the way down to Canopus, Manning put in a call for Angus McBlla and when he arrived at the spaceport the guide was already waiting for him.

"I want to go to twenty-seven Circle Square," he told the guide. "You know where it is?"

"Nothing to it," Angus said as he hailed an aircab. He chuckled as they climbed in. "You know, Circle Square created quite a stir when the Canopusians first started trying to interest the rest of the universe in coming here by sending out pamphlets. But the attraction died as soon as the first bunch of galactic scholars arrived."

"Why?" Manning asked.

"Well, the sales literature of the Chamber of Commerce gave the impression that the Canopusians, in building Circle Square, had finally managed to square a circle. But all they had actually done was build the street on two levels. The first level was a square and the second level was a circle."

"Clever, these Canopusians," Manning said dryly.

Within a few minutes, Angus guiding the driver, the aircab set down on the upper level of Circle Square and let them out. Angus pointed out number 27 and once more went to a sense-lounge to wait for his client.

THE OFFICE of the Marital Relations Bureau turned out to be a lavish place. The lighting was subtle, giving the impression of being standard romance lighting. Actually, Manning soon realized, the combination was an exaggeration of the usual lighting guaranteed to stimulate romantic emotions. As a result, he guessed, a few minutes in the reception room could almost be certain to turn genuine love to hate. He also suspected that there was an antagonist perfume being sprayed into the room, but he could not be certain.

The receptionist was a Canopusian. She took Manning's name and asked him to wait. She made a couple of attempts to get him to talking about his problems, but gave up when she had no success.

It was about fifteen minutes before she told Manning he could go in. She indicated the door back of her desk and he went through, into one of the most luxurious offices he had ever seen. Everything in it, in terms of color and lighting, had been planned to establish trust in the occupant. Again, Manning thought he caught a faint scent of one of the dependency perfumes,[24] but it was so slight he couldn't, swear to it.

Nottyl Nadyl was short and fat. He was no more than four feet tall, but his rounded body was almost as wide as the desk behind which he sat. His head was another, smaller balloon. He was partly bald, but a luxurious growth of coarse hair sprouted from the back of his head, hanging halfway down his back. A broad smile crinkled the flesh up around his four eyes, giving him a jolly appearance.

"Come in, come in," he called as Manning stopped in the doorway. "Welcome to the Marital Relations Bureau of Canopus—the refuge of bruised spirits, the home of last resorts. Come in, sir."

Manning took the chair in front of the desk and examined

---

24 The entire line of Hypno-Perfumes had, of course, been banned throughout the galaxy in 2963, after the scandal caused by the Crunchy Suit Company spraying an entire planet just before they started a planet-wide visicast campaign to unload an inventory of shoddy clothes. It was rumored, however, that a few companies still used the perfumes, adulterated with some new chemical that made it almost impossible to detect them without the most delicate of instruments.

the creature who beamed at him. He remembered that J. Barnaby had said Nadyl was an Algolian. Manning had met a number of Algolians. He was certain that Angus McBlla, the guide, was also from Algol—but Nadyl seemed to be from a different race than any of the others he'd seen.

"I am Nottyl Nadyl, at your service," the Algolian said. "No marital problem too difficult for us. Your name, sir?" He still smiled broadly, but his eyes were studying Manning with a humorless gaze.

"Melvin Draco," said Manning. He was certain the Algolian already knew his name.

"And how did you happen to seek our services, Mr. Draco?"

"You sent me a letter," Manning said, pulling it from his pocket.

"We send out so many letters," murmured Nadyl. "So there is a rift in your conjugal bliss—did you find it difficult to understand me, Mr. Draco? Should I speak more simply?"

"Of course, I understand you; I'm hardly an idiot," Manning said irritably.

"Of course not," the Algolian said hastily, but his voice lacked conviction. "You are a Terran?"

"I'm a Terran." Manning was beginning to wonder what some of these aliens on Canopus thought Terrans were like; this was the second time he'd been asked doubtfully about his origin. He checked the impulse to look to see if his clothing was disarranged. For a minute he felt like the man at whom the famous Tongue-Shrinker ads[25] were aimed.

WHATEVER IT WAS that was disturbing the Algolian, he dismissed it. "Well," he said briskly, "what seems to be your problem, Mr. Draco?"

"My wife," Manning said solemnly, "is a very beautiful woman

---

25 "Do you maintain sophisticated poise in all circumstances, or are you often embarrassed by lack of Tongue Control? When you see something you want and can't have, does your tongue hang out? If so, buy Meehel's Patented Tongue-Shrinker."

and I am quite fond of her. But the poor woman has a most unpleasant voice which she uses almost constantly. And lately she seems to have decided that a husband's place is across the room from his wife."

"A most unfortunate situation," the Algolian agreed pleasantly. His tentacles busied themselves with things on the desk in a manner reminding Manning of J. Barnaby Cruikshank. "We find it to be, however, a rather common complaint. But not one, I might add, which offers any obstacles to our services."

"Just how do you work?" Manning asked.

"As stated in my letter, there is no charge for consultation. If I succeed—and I have *never* failed, Mr. Draco—in eliminating your problem, there will be a charge of one hundred credits."

"That seems fair enough."

"But," the Algolian said, "you must follow *all* of my recommendations to the letter."

Manning squirmed in his seat, giving a good imitation of a man who wants to be sure of something but doesn't know how to approach it. "The—ah—treatment is permanent?" he asked.

"Oh, decidedly permanent," the Algolian said cheerfully.

Manning peered at the letter again, then glanced hesitatingly at Nadyl. "I was especially interested in this sentence in your letter which refers to the possibility of—ah—making a profit...."

"I'm glad you mentioned that," Nadyl said. "It is always a pleasure to do business with a practical man. Do you carry insurance, Mr. Draco?"

"Only a small policy on myself...."

"Insurance," the Algolian said sententiously, "is one of the wisest investments a man can make. I suggest that at your earliest opportunity you take out a joint policy covering yourself and your wife. A policy for not less than one hundred thousand credits. One never knows when the Grim Reaper may snatch away a beloved and it is well to be financially prepared for such events."

"I suppose so," Manning said dutifully.

"We trust, of course, that you and your wife will both enjoy the fruits of longevity, but in the event of any untoward fatality to your wife I suggest that you deal with the Happy Asteroid Mortuary here on Canopus. The owner, Encycla Grave, is from my own planet and I can assure you that he operates with the utmost tact. He will handle all details for a quiet burial on an asteroid, which will then be power-driven out into space, leaving no trace of—er—your recent bereavement. Although he is rather expensive, he is worth it."

"How expensive?"

"Fifty percent of the amount of the policy on your wife," the Algolian said. "This may seem large until you consider the extent of his services and the fact that there is still a comfortable margin between the amount you retain and the one-year premium you will have paid."

"Let me get this straight," Manning said bluntly. His forehead was wrinkled with thought. "If I take out an insurance policy for a hundred thousand credits or more, and if I agree to give half of it to this undertaker fellow, then you'll kill my wife. Is that it?"

The Algolian threw up his tentacles in horror. "My dear fellow," he exclaimed, "must you talk like a character on a visiscreen thriller? Rather let us put it this way: You have a marital problem. Your wife's present attitude and actions are an obstacle to your complete happiness. I am an individual who is deeply concerned about the happiness of everyone. If, therefore, you agree to follow all of my various suggestions, I will undertake to eliminate the things which stand in the way of your happiness. There is, you understand, no guarantee of anything; neither is there any cost to you until you have had your present discomfort alleviated."

"You certainly do a lot of talking to say something that's pretty simple," Manning observed. "But I guess that's your way, so we'll leave it at that."

"Good," said the Algolian. "You may put your trust in me, Mr. Draco. Good day, sir."

"I'll wait to hear from you," Manning said.

CHAPTER FOUR

B ACK ON THE ASTEROID, there was nothing to do but wait. Under the circumstances, that wasn't easy. During the day, Manning went down to the hunting lodge. There wasn't anything to hunt, but he didn't mind. The idea was to get away from Fanya. The lodge was equipped with a number of devices to amuse the idle rich, but most of these were of an erotic nature so he ignored them, since they would only lead his thoughts back to the blonde. In the evening, he usually tried to escape to his room and watch the visicasts. To stay in the same room with the blonde too long was a mistake; he'd soon find himself wanting to defy science.

The morning after his visit to the marriage counselor, Manning and Fanya had their first visitors. A U-pilot ship drifted in and set down on the small port in front of the house. The hatch swung open and two individuals stepped out. One of them was a nondescript Terran; the other was an Algolian, but of still a different species.

Despite his bulky size and the usual three legs,[26] he was roughly humanoid in appearance. His head was shaped very much like that of a human. It was completely bald and there were two eyes in front and two in the rear. The slight similarity was helped by the fact that the lower part of his face was encased in a bushy beard. The beard seemed to have a life of its own, indicating that the hairs were sense organs.

---

26   In the small amount of literature on the subject, it had been noted that there were always three identical features about Algolians, although everything else might be different. These were the three legs, the four eyes, and that any hairs on their bodies were invariably sense organs. But because no one had yet seen two Algolians who looked alike, these features were about the only way of identifying natives of that planet.

The visitors turned out to be Sam Warren and Jaba Woo, the representatives of the Greater Solarian Insurance Company, Monopolated. They pretended to have dropped by accidentally and Manning gave no indication that he had other thoughts on the subject.

After considerable idle chatter, the subject of insurance came up. Manning admitted that he might be in the market for some and inquired about joint policies. It just happened that the two insurance salesmen had come equipped for his special problems and it wasn't long before Mr. and Mrs. Melvin Draco were each insured for two hundred thousand credits. Manning had decided to double the minimum suggested by Nadyl on the grounds that this might make him more eager.

"The place," he said to Fanya when the two happy insurance salesmen had left, "is lousy with Algolians. I wonder what the fourth one will look like?"

"Are you going to see him?" Fanya asked.

Manning shook his head. "All I was told was that I should secure his services if anything happened to you. It might be unseemly if I were to go hire an undertaker in advance."

The blonde giggled.

"Are you sure," Manning asked with concern, "that you're not going to be in any danger?"

"Positive," she said. "There are ways, of course, that he could kill me, but they all require personal contact and the device Mr. Cruikshank gave me will protect me from that as well as from what you have in mind… but you must hurry, Manning."

"I'll hurry," he said. "And I resent the use of the word 'protect' in connection with my intentions. I'll make you eat that word."

"Any time," she said softly.

Manning thrust his hands deeply into his pockets so that they wouldn't get ideas of their own. "In the meantime," he said savagely, "we have to wait it out."

AND WAIT THEY DID, but not too long. That night there was a call for Manning over a closed circuit on the visiscreen and a clerk in the Milky Way Union read a spacegram to him. It was from Nottyl Nadyl and merely said: "I suggest that tomorrow you make an early visit to your hunting lodge." That was all.

Early the following morning, Manning went to the hunting lodge. Despite Fanya's assurance, he was a little nervous about leaving her there to face whatever the jolly Algolian counselor had in mind. He grew even more fidgety when he heard a small ship landing near the house. He almost held his breath, waiting for the next step.

When it came he almost jumped out of his chair. It was the rapid firing of a subatomic gun, guaranteed to bring down anything up to a Marfakian Lair-Lizard which weighed seventy tons. It hardly seemed possible that a frail creature like the blonde could withstand a round of shots from that gun.

Manning ran from the lodge and dashed frantically toward the house, the light gravity of the asteroid permitting him to cover twenty feet at a leap. Even so, he was no more than halfway to the house when he saw a small ship leaving the asteroid with a rush.

Reaching the house, he ran into the living room and stopped, horrified at what he saw. Fanya Sera was sprawled on the floor. The room and a good portion of the furniture had been wrecked by the shots that had been fired.

He was shocked out of his grief by the sound of soft laughter. Then Fanya was sitting up, smiling at him.

"You're not hurt?" he asked in astonishment.

"Not at all," she said. "I just thought it more dramatic to fall this way and let him think he had killed me. Oh, I may have a few small bruises, but that'll be all. See."

She opened the front of her dress and stood up. There were a series of small red spots, running from her navel to her collarbone, but so far as he could see, that was all the damage. Knowing that she was unharmed, however, Manning found it difficult to confine his gaze to the region of the bruises.

The blonde laughed again and slowly closed her dress.

"Now what do we do?" she asked.

"Ordinarily that would be a stupid question," Manning said dryly. "As it is, however, we merely wait until Mr. Nadyl has time to get back to his office and then I will call and tell him that he's failed. That ought to throw him into enough of a panic so things will get interesting."

They waited, but not as long as they had expected to. Manning was just about to go make his call when they heard a ship coming in to land. A moment later, there was a soft note from the door announcer. Manning went and threw it open.

The fourth Algolian stood there. He was all of eight feet tall, his body not much thicker than a man's leg. Again there were the three legs and the four eyes, but they were quite different in appearance from those of the others. And this one, Manning noticed when he turned partly sideways, had his hair in the back, looking somewhat like a rooster's tail. He was dressed entirely in black and there was a solemn expression on his thin face.

"Mr. Melvin Draco?" he asked in a melancholy voice.

"Yes," Manning said.

"I regret to intrude upon your moment of tragedy, Mr. Draco, but there are certain traditions we must carry on, painful though they be. But I want you to know that my heart goes out to you in your hour of grief and I stand ready to remove much of the burden from your shoulders."

"Who are you?" Manning asked.

"Encycla Grave, of the Happy Asteroid Mortuary. Now there are a few trifling—" He caught a glimpse of Fanya in the background and broke off. "Ah, I see there is someone with you. A relative, perhaps...."

"Oh, that's my wife," Manning said.

THERE WAS sheer amazement on the Algolian's face. "Surely you jest, sir? It is hardly possible you could have remarried so quickly, to say nothing of the fact that it would be in extremely bad taste—"

"But I haven't remarried." Manning said patiently. "This is my only wife. We arrived from Terra only a few days ago. Now what was it you wanted to see me about?"

"I don't understand," the Algolian said in some agitation. "Your wife—oh, dear, this *is* terrible. You must excuse me...." He turned and ran for his ship, his long legs twinkling over the ground. It took him only a minute to reach it and then the ship was lancing up into the sky.

Inside the house, Manning and Fanya laughed together.

"He'll report back to his friend, the happiness boy," Manning said, "and by the time I call, Mr. Nadyl's nerves should be in a fine state. Or maybe I'll beat him to it."

He started for the other room, only to be called back by the blonde. "There's another ship coming in," she said.

Manning listened and heard it. He came back to stand beside her. "Who do you suppose is interested in your corpse now?"

They heard the ship ease to the ground and cut to silence. Then a moment later, the door announcer sounded again. Manning strode across the room and flung open the door.

This time it was a Terran who stood there. He was a tall man, lean of frame and hard of eye. His clothes were a little old-fashioned, as was the snap-brim hat he wore. His gaze bored into Manning's.

"I'm Mickey Hatchet," he said in a clipped voice.

Manning nodded, surprised. He was familiar with the name.[27]

---

27 So was everybody else in the galaxy who ever watched the visicasts. Once every week, year in and year out, Mickey Hatchet waded through gallons of gore and over the bodies of beautiful babes for the entertainment of untold billions. But few people knew the full story of Mickey Hatchet. In the beginning he had been merely the creation of a writer named Spunky Malone—the last of the private detectives. But over the years, as he grew more and more popular, the author began to identify himself with the character he had created. Finally, Spunky Malone had his name legally changed to Mickey Hatchet. Then he arranged to have all the visifilms done in half of each year; the other half, Mickey Hatchet roamed the universe (he owned the only private detective license in existence by this time), fighting evil where he found it and trying to make this a better universe in which to live. It was a one-sided battle, but there was nothing that could

"My name is Draco," Manning said. "This is Mrs. Draco."

Mickey Hatchet's gaze raked over the blonde. There was something in his eyes that said he might have been interested if there had only been time.

"Caught the vibrations of some shots," he said. "What's the caper?"

"Shots? Caper?" Manning said. "I'm afraid I don't know what you mean. My wife and I were just sitting here talking."

Mickey Hatchet shoved past him into the room. He looked around, taking in the damaged furniture and walls. His gaze raked over the body of the blonde.

"You and your wife must've had some pretty hard words," he said. He strode over and grabbed Manning by the shoulders. "I don't like it," he said. "Something's going on here. It's in the air. I can smell it."

"Nothing that I can't handle." Manning said, stepping out of his grip.

"Look," said Mickey Hatchet. "I'm in this. To the finish. I don't like being in it any better than you would. But that's the way it is. There are a lot of alley cats in this universe, who'll do anything for a fast credit; they don't care whose blood it is. But it's my universe, too. I'd like it to be a clean place to live and I'm going to see that it is. You understand that?"

"I think so," Manning said.

"Okay." Mickey Hatchet's gaze raked over the blonde again. He saw that the zipper on her dress hadn't been pulled all the way to the top. He pointed a bony finger and whirled on Manning. "The broad had her dress open?"

"Yes," Manning admitted.

"And she's wearing nothing under it?"

"Y-yes. But—"

"Happens to me all the time," Mickey Hatchet said wearily. He pointed the finger again, this time at her middle. "There's

---

make Mickey Hatchet swerve from the firmness of his purpose—nothing.

only one thing to do. Pow!" He turned and strode toward the door.

"Wait a minute," Manning said. "There is something you might be able to do."

"You want a little private eye work, you've come to the right place. What?"

"Pretty soon there'll be another ship coming here. When it leaves, it'll leave in a hurry. Think you can tail it?"

"I'll tail him so close you'll think I grew on his back," said Mickey Hatchet.

"How do I get in touch with you?" Manning asked.

"Call my ship. The *Trigger Happy.*"

Fanya murmured something in her own tongue,[28] but neither man paid any attention.

"All right," Manning said. "I'll get in touch with you later."

"I'll be around," Mickey Hatchet said. He turned and slammed out of the house. A moment later his ship took off as though it had a burr under its rockets.

"I've heard a lot about him," Manning said. He looked at the blonde with curiosity. "Tell me, did you have any urge to rip your dress off while he was in the room?"

"No, but I do now," she said. One hand went to the zipper on her dress.

"Not now," Manning said hastily and fled to the other room.

MANNING PUT IN a call to Nottyl Nadyl. The latter's face, when it appeared on the screen, was not as jolly as it had been the last time Manning had seen it. It was impossible to tell since there was no color on the screen, but Manning thought his face looked a little green. The undertaker must have already been in touch with him.

"What kind of a bungler are you?" Manning demanded. "My wife is still alive."

"I don't understand it," the Algolian said. A ray of hope

---

28 What she'd said was, "If a man answers, hang up."

struggled into his face. "I don't suppose the accident has changed your mind—made you realize that the bonds of matrimony are more precious than you thought?"

"Certainly not," snapped Manning. "I made a bargain and I expect you to fulfill it."

The Algolian sighed heavily. "Very well. I suggest that you go back to the hunting lodge. I shall be there shortly and this time I guarantee that nothing will go wrong."

"It better not," Manning said and broke the connection.

He told Fanya to get set for another visit, then went on down to the lodge. This time he felt less restless, but he sat by a window where he could watch the house.

It wasn't long before he saw the ship coming in. But instead of landing as it had before, it merely swooped low over the house. Then it went into a steep, rapid climb. Immediately afterward there was an explosion that rocked the lodge.

Manning hadn't expected a bomb and his old fears returned. He ran for the house as rapidly as he could. Even as he ran, however, he saw a second ship dart out from behind a distant asteroid and take out after the first one.

When he reached the house, it wasn't necessary to open the door. While the rest of the house was intact, what had once been the living room was only smoking rubble. That meant a controlled oxygen bomb, one of the most deadly weapons known to the civilized galaxy.

And there in the center of the rubble, her dress scorched and in tatters, stood Fanya Sera. She laughed at the sight of Manning's face.

When he was finally convinced that she was unharmed—he'd started to pinch her to make certain but a warning tremor had proved the ultrasonic device was equally indestructible—he relaxed.

"I think that'll be the last attempt," he told her. "I want to make sure that Nadyl knows he's failed again. Then I'm going down to Canopus and clean this up while they're still in a panic."

He went into his room and put in a call to Nadyl's office. He left a message with the Canopusian receptionist. Then he rejoined the blonde.

"I'm on my way," he said. He noticed that, if anything, the damaged condition of her dress made her even more appealing. "I don't suppose you'd care to shut that gadget off long enough to give me a kiss for luck?"

"I'd like to, but I won't," she said.

"I thought you wouldn't," he said with a sigh. "Well, by the time I come back it'll all be over."

"I'll be waiting for you in your room," she said. There was even more promise in the quality of her voice than there was in the words.

"With the lights out?" he asked with a grin.

"With the lights out," she said solemnly. "You can turn them on later, if you like, but they'll be out when you arrive."

He pretended to catch the kiss she threw and tuck it in his pocket. Then he went down to his ship.

CHAPTER FIVE

ON THE WAY down to Canopus, Manning put in a call to the guide he had used before. He wanted to be able to move fast and he knew that he wouldn't be able to get anywhere without a guide. His call was taken by an answering service, but the girl assured him that Angus McBlla would be at the spaceport by the time Manning was.

He was, too. Manning explained to him the places he wanted to go and they started out in an aircab.

The first stop was at the hotel where Jaba Woo lived. He wasn't in and he hadn't been all day. Sam Warren lived at the same hotel, so Manning dropped in there. The little Terran claimed he didn't know where his Algolian partner was. He told Manning that Jaba Woo was supposed to have been there an hour earlier so that they could keep an appointment with a client, but he hadn't even called. His concern seemed to be sincere.

Manning picked up his guide in the hotel's sense-lounge and they went on to the Happy Asteroid Mortuary. The building was an imposing structure, designed in the shape of an asteroid. There were a number of employees around, mostly Canopusians, but no Encycla Grave. By questioning the employees, Manning discovered that he hadn't been there since some time before he had called at Manning's rented asteroid.

By this time, Manning was expecting the pattern to be repeated. Nevertheless, he went to Circle Square and the office of the Marital Relations Bureau. The Canopusian receptionist was there. So were two clients. But that was all. The receptionist had no idea what was delaying Mr. Nadyl. She suggested that Manning sit down and wait with the other two men.

By this time, Manning was convinced that his hunch was right. He went over to the sense-lounge where Angus McBlla was waiting and used the public visibooth to put in a call to Terra. When J. Barnaby Cruikshank showed up on the screen, he quickly reported what had been going on.

"I think," he said, "that Nadyl must have realized that the bomb also failed to kill Fanya. Probably had a ground scanner in his ship. That must have made him realize it was a trap. He notified the other two and they all started looking for a hole. I'm hoping that Mickey Hatchet will have something for me on Nadyl. Otherwise it may be tough."

"What about Sam Warren and this Dzanku?" J. Barnaby asked.

"I haven't seen Dzanku and I think Sam Warren's in the clear."

"I don't pay you to think," snapped J. Barnaby. "I'm telling you they have to be mixed up in it. Check that Rigelian."

"All right," Manning said. "In the meantime, I'm going to come out in the open. That'll let me check a lot of angles I've had to stay away from as long as I was supposed to be a tourist."

"Dig up everything you can," said J. Barnaby. "But I think you've got enough evidence to make the beginnings of a case. We don't want them slipping through our fingers. I'm going to tell the Federation police to issue pick-up orders on all five of them. Maybe they'll be in custody by the time you've finished checking."

"Maybe," Manning said doubtfully.

"How are you getting along with Fanya?" J. Barnaby asked. There was something suspiciously like a chuckle in his voice.

"You know how I'm getting along with her," Manning said darkly. "But I'll soon wash up this case and then it'll be a different story."

"When you've finished this case," J. Barnaby said sternly, "I order you to come directly home. I forbid you to take any time to play around with that blonde. I—"

"Get lost," Manning said and cut the connection.

HE COLLECTED his guide and they went looking for the second-hand asteroid dealer. They found him in his little office. It turned out that he, too, was looking for the Algolian undertaker. The latter had bought a crypt-asteroid from him the day before, but hadn't yet paid for it.

"You think he's skipped out?" Dzanku asked Manning.

"I don't know," Manning said evasively. "Why should he skip? He has a successful business. I wouldn't think he'd walk out on that."

"I don't know," the Rigelian said. "You can never tell…."

"You think he's mixed up in something crooked?"

"I didn't say that."

"You did a lot of business with him?" Manning asked.

"Yes."

"How did he pay you in the past?"

"Always in cash," Dzanku said. He hesitated, then went on. "As a matter of fact, Mr. Draco, that's why I was a little suspicious of him. You take an established businessman, when he always pays in cash you begin to wonder how established he is. It looks like he might always be ready to move fast."

"I see what you mean," Manning said. "By the way, did you ever have any dealings with a Nottyl Nadyl?"

The Rigelian looked thoughtful, then shook his head. "I don't remember anyone by that name."

"What about Jaba Woo?"

Again the Rigelian shook his head.

His three eyes peered intently at Manning. "Both of them Algolians?" he asked.

Manning nodded.

"I don't know them," Dzanku said, "but if it means anything you can be sure they know each other. All Algolians have a very close relationship."

They talked some more and Manning had the distinct impression that the Rigelian was leveling with him. He had an impulse to warn him that the police would soon be after him, but suppressed it.

After leaving Dzanku, Manning found another public visibooth. He asked the operator to locate the ship *Trigger Happy*. It took about five minutes, but finally the voice of Mickey Hatchet answered. The screen, however, remained blank.

"This is Draco," Manning said. "Why aren't you using video?"

"Can't," came the cryptic answer. "That would get me in real trouble."

"What about that ship you were tailing?" Manning asked.

"Better not report on this hook-up," Mickey Hatchet said grimly. "Come to my ship and I'll fill you in."

"Where are you?"

"Six-two over three-zero at forty thousand feet."

Muttering his opinion of the universe's last private eye, Manning left the booth. He picked up Angus McBlla and back they went to the spaceport. Ordering Angus to wait, Manning went up in his own ship. He soon found Mickey Hatchet's ship. He edged in next to it, switched on the grappling magnet, and a few minutes later was stepping through the hatch of the other ship.

THEN HE FOUND OUT why Mickey Hatchet had refused to use video. He wasn't alone. There was a lush-looking red-headed Terran girl with him. Manning had no trouble appreciating her best points, for she wore no clothing at all.

"A friend of yours?" Manning said.

"Ahh," said Mickey Hatchet, making a sound of disgust in his throat. The girl had edged closer to him and he reached out and gave her a shove.

"Hon-ey," she said plaintively in protest. Her voice came from the back of her throat and sounded like she was in the grip of a personal emotional crisis.

"I hate to intrude on your love life," Manning said dryly, "but I would like to know about that ship you were tailing."

"Sure. That guy that bombed your place, he barreled out of there like a shot. But I was on his tail and stuck there as close as a bill collector... get out of here." The last was to the redhead, who was edging up again.

"Hon-ey," the girl said.

"Dames," said Mickey Hatchet in disgust. "Anyway, there we were—cutting around through that asteroid field like a couple of kids playing hide-and-seek. And all the time this dame was a stowaway on my ship—beat it, baby."

"Hon-ey," the girl said.

"Scram out of here," Mickey Hatchet said to the redhead. "I'm trying to talk to the man."

"Hon-ey," the girl said, starting to edge up again.

"I'll plow you," Mickey Hatchet spat. The girl didn't stop. Mickey Hatchet drew a gun, leveled it and pulled the trigger. The girl fell to the floor, twitched a few times, and then was quiet.[29] There was a hole in her belly and the blood was oozing

---

29　Mickey Hatchet was actually not as harmful as it might seem. The only thing that made him trigger happy was the attention of undraped females. Very few

out. Mickey Hatchet used his foot to slide the body into the escape hatch. He kicked a lever and the body shot out into space. "The garbage detail can pick her up tomorrow," he said. He patted his gun. "This is the one thing that never fails me in handling those dames. Now, where was I?"

"Playing hide-and-seek, I think," Manning said. He had been fascinated by the little drama he'd watched. He'd heard about this side of Mickey Hatchet's life, but this was the first time he'd seen it in action.

"Yeah. Like I said, I was barreling after this guy when suddenly that dame appeared. With nothing on, just as you saw. Really stacked, too, if you know what I mean, but I was busy. I told her to get lost. Then she came over and sat right down on my lap. I was trying to figure out what her game was, and wondering if I should just sap her, and while that was going on I lost that guy. He dodged behind one of those asteroids and by the time I could get the dame off my lap and get straightened out, he was gone."

"All right," Manning said with a sigh. He knew there was no point in saying what he thought. "That's the way it goes sometimes. Stick around, Mickey, and I'll let you know the score."

"You want me to go down and smoke them out?"

"No, you stay here. Just circle around until you hear from me." Manning went back to his own ship. His last glimpse of Mickey Hatchet, the private eye was shaking his head. "Dames," he was saying.

When he got back to the spaceport, he had his program all mapped out. With Angus McBlla guiding him, he made the rounds, starting with space customs, then the local banks, and

---

girls had conducted themselves in this manner for years, if they ever had, so they were fairly safe. The redhead was, in truth, a cleverly made robot. The producer of the Mickey Hatchet visiscreen show had a number of these robots made up each year and planted in strategic spots. They were activated by Mickey Hatchet's presence. He never knew the truth of the matter, but the robots did a lot to keep him happy.

a number of business houses. When he'd finished, he had collected some interesting facts.

JABA WOO was the only Algolian who had officially entered Canopus. He was also the only one of the three who had a bank account. Both Nottyl Nadyl and Encycla Grave had paid cash for everything they bought. What was even more interesting was that he could find no resident address for either Nadyl or Grave. Jaba Woo had made large deposits coinciding with each one of the deaths in the insurance cases. He had also made large withdrawals, but he still had a very comfortable balance. He hadn't been to the bank to close the account, but he had made a visicall, asking the bank to transfer his account to the First Galactic Bank on Pictor. Manning arrived at the bank just in time. As Chief Investigator for Greater Solarian he also had police powers, so the transfer was stopped.

The spaceport officials were certain that no one—especially an Algolian—had left the planet. Yet the three Algolians had managed to vanish completely, unless the police had been able to find them. Quite obviously they had been ready to vanish the minute anything went wrong with their racket. And the minute Nadyl had realized that "Mrs. Draco" was an indestructible, he had flashed the word that the game was up.

"Angus," Manning said to the guide as they left the bank, "did you know Jaba Woo, Nottyl Nadyl, and Encycla Grave?"

"I knew them," the guide said. "Not well, you understand."

"I thought that all Algolians maintained a very close relationship. That's what I was told."

"True up to a point," the guide admitted. "But you have to consider the class differences. The ones you mention were all businessmen while I am a mere guide. They would have considered it degrading to be too friendly with me."

They walked past a corner where some workers were excavating for a new building. The blasting was being done with ultrasonics. Manning could hear nothing, although it was strong enough to make him aware of pressure on his nerves. But he noticed that Angus McBlla's face contorted with pain. The knot of hair on his head momentarily lost its mushroom shape, seemed to be almost trying to move over to the side of his face away from the blasting. Then they were past the corner and the sensitive hearing-hair resumed its shape.

"You know that I'm trying to find them," Manning said. "Would you have any idea where they've gone?"

The guide shook his head. "Algolians are very hard to find," he said, "when they wish not to be found. Maybe they've left Canopus."

"I don't think so," Manning said. "Well, there are a few other things I want to check, but first take me to the headquarters of the Federation police."

"Sure thing," the guide said cheerfully. "It's not far; we might as well walk."

They had almost reached the police station when Manning had a bright idea. He stopped off at a public visibooth and put in a call to the Solar University on Mars. He was in the booth for a long time, but when he emerged he looked a little more cheerful.

"Did you find them?" the waiting guide asked.

"No," Manning said. "That was a personal call."

When they reached the police station, Angus McBlla was about to head for the nearest sense-lounge, but Manning stopped him. "I'll only be in here long enough to find out if they know anything," he said. "Then we'll go on. You might as well go in with me. You'll get loaded if you keep waiting for me in those joints."

Angus grinned and followed him inside.

LEAVING THE GUIDE waiting in the outer office, Manning went in to see the Sector Commander. The police had picked up Sam Warren and Dzanku Dzanku, both of whom were loudly protesting their innocence, but there was no clue to the three Algolians. The police had also duplicated most of Manning's investigations. Dzanku had a comfortable bank account, but there was no related pattern between his deposits and the insurance crimes. Sam Warren not only had no bank account, but had already hocked his future commissions.

Manning borrowed a small sonic-gun from the Sector Commander. He set it at the lowest intensity and slipped it in his pocket. The Commander walked into the outer office with him.

As they approached Angus McBlla, Manning put his hand in his pocket, tipped the sonic-gun, and triggered it.

The Algolian stiffened with the shock, then his flesh moved with a speed that was blinding to watch. The sharp corners of his body blurred and rounded. The flesh on his head writhed, the eyes moving frantically, the antennae-like hair moving down his back.

Manning turned off the sonic-gun. "There," he said, "is our *three* Algolians."

The guide was rapidly resuming his original shape, but the police had stepped in and quickly put force-cuffs on him before they allowed themselves the luxury of curiosity. They were trained to act first and check the accuracy of their actions later.

"Now, would you explain?" said the Commander.

"Sure," Manning said. He indicated the guide, whose four eyes were staring angrily at him. "That's Angus McBlla, alias Nottyl Nadyl, alias Encycla Grave, alias Jaba Woo. When he came here, he merely set himself up as four different Algolians, each one looking different. I should have tumbled to it right away. The officials at the spaceport told me that only one Algolian was officially on this planet. Then Jaba Woo was the only one who had a bank account and a residential address. Three of his four personalities were involved in the racket, but the fourth one wasn't. When things started going wrong, he merely made the three vanish. Then as the guide, the unsuspected one, he trotted around with me. That way he could keep an eye on what was happening."

"But," asked the bewildered official, "how could he manage to look entirely different in each case?"

"I had a hunch," Manning said. "All we've ever known about Algolians is that no two have ever been seen that looked alike. Today, when Angus and I passed a spot where they were doing some sonic blasting, I thought I saw his hair and flesh move as though trying to get away from it. At first, I thought it was my imagination. But then I decided to give my imagination the benefit of the doubt. I called the Solar University and talked to a specialist in alien life. I suggested that he think of Algolians having psycho-adaptable flesh. He got pretty excited.

"They have discovered life that can change its appearance, but they just hadn't thought of that in connection with Algolians. He said that would explain everything. The Algolians are known to be strongly individualistic; he said if they were able to change their appearance at will, they would probably choose to look different from their fellow Algolians. He suggested that I try a sonic-gun on one of them and if he started to change appearance, then I was on the right track. You saw what happened."

"Take him away," the Commander ordered. Several of his men led the Algolian back in the direction of the cells.

"Now I need a visiphone," Manning told the Commander.

He was led into a private office and left alone. He put in a call to J. Barnaby and briefly reported.

"Good boy," J. Barnaby said when he'd finished. "I knew I could depend on you to clean it up."

"Just one more thing," Manning said. "Neither Sam Warren nor Dzanku Dzanku was really mixed up in it. I know you can probably press charges against them, since to some extent they were used by the Algolian, but I suggest you drop them."

CRUIKSHANK SHOOK his head. "They were accessories after the fact, even in the best light. No, they'll have to be charged with that. Maybe I'll see to it that they're let off with a fine providing they contract to pay off our losses. If they do that I'll keep Warren on and maybe give that Rigelian a job and take it out of their commissions."

Manning argued with him some more, but there was no

moving J. Barnaby Cruikshank once he'd made up his mind. Manning finally gave up in disgust.

"Another thing," he said. "Are you keeping your word with Fanya?"

"Of course," J. Barnaby said. "I never break my word. But I'm ordering you to stay away from her."

Manning told him what he could do with his orders.

"Manning, my boy," J. Barnaby said, "I—"

Draco broke the connection. He was in a hurry to get back to the asteroid, but first he got permission to see Sam Warren and Dzanku.

The Terran and the Rigelian were both in a single cell. They were a sorry-looking pair. Manning first told them about the Algolian and what had been going on.

"He actually was pretty stupid," he finished. "I don't know why he wasn't caught long before."

"You're wrong, you know," Dzanku, the Rigelian, said. "I didn't know what was going on, but I can tell you that you are probably the only Terran who could have set a trap for him with any success."

"What do you mean?" Manning asked.

"Algolians are mind-readers," Dzanku said, "even as are we Rigelians. They have, however, a very strong secondary mind shield, so that I never could see deeply into his mind. But I know that he would have been able to read the intentions of any other Terran."

"Why couldn't he read my mind, then?"

"I'm not too sure. Haven't you ever been given a cybernetic M-R?"

"Many times," Manning said. Then he remembered the peculiar business at the hospital and told the Rigelian about it.

"That must be it," Dzanku said. "Your accident did something that gave you a secondary mind shield—only you are unable to control it, so that it's like a permanent block. I was surprised myself when I met you. It's not like a legitimate mind shield. As a matter of fact, my first impression was that you merely had a very shallow mind—not very bright."

Manning remembered the way "Nadyl" had acted, asking if Manning was able to understand him. It was the way he would have treated someone he considered a moron.

"That's why you were able to trap him," Dzanku said. "He thought you weren't very bright and so he never became suspicious." He studied Manning a minute. "You probably have the beginnings of a genuine mind shield there—thanks to your accident. You ought to take some time off and go to Rigel. We have some excellent mind-trainers there and they might be able to teach you."

"But in the meantime, what about us?" Sam Warren asked sourly.

Manning told them about his conversation with J. Barnaby. He said he'd try to argue with him again, but that he doubted that it would do any good. Sam Warren was pretty downcast by the news, but Dzanku seemed to take it in his stride.

"I expected it," he said. "As a matter of fact, I guess I was foolish ever to think I could get away with being honest. My own people turned against me and no one else would ever believe that I was honest. Believe me, I've learned my lesson. Honesty doesn't pay. I've already been in touch with my home planet and I'll get some help from them—since they're convinced that I've reformed." His eye-stalks bent toward Sam Warren. "I think I can help Sam, too."

"Well, I'll try again," Manning said. "In the meantime, I've got to run along. I've got a heavy date with a blonde."

HE HAD REACHED the cell door before the Rigelian stopped him.

"One minute," said Dzanku. "I appreciate your attitude toward me in this matter, Mr. Draco. I think I might do one more good deed before I completely reform. You won't mind a bit of advice?"

"Of course not," Manning said. He was puzzled, but waited patiently.

"The blonde you're rushing off to see," Dzanku said. "Is that the lady who was posing as your wife, the one that was indestructible?"

"Yes."

"I believe you mentioned that she's from Alioth?"

"Yes."

The Rigelian sighed heavily. "I don't suppose you'll thank me until later, but didn't you know that Aliothan females are restricted to their own planets? They are only allowed off when there are certain precautions taken, and even then it takes a lot of political pull to arrange it."

"She told me about the restrictions," Manning said impatiently. "I gathered it has something to do with the Aliothan women being subjected by the men."

"The restrictions are imposed by the Federation," Dzanku said. "Aliothans are evolved from a form of life known on your Terra as Narbonne Lycosa, or *Lycosa narbonnensis.* Oh, they are highly evolved, having assumed humanoid shape and all, but they have retained a few of the instincts of their ancestors."

"What are you trying to say?" Manning demanded.

"The Narbonne Lycosa was a spider," Dzanku said gently. "The female of the species always killed and ate the male immediately after breeding. The Aliothan women have retained this trait. Aliothan males have become too submissive for their taste. The only time that females can be taken away from their planet is when they are about ready for mating. They'll mate with any humanoid male and find aliens very attractive. So they will agree to any terms so long as it will finally give them a little free time to mate—and then eat. You've been here for several days now, so I imagine that your blonde is very eager—and very hungry."

Manning had a sudden memory of the eager look in Fanya's eyes and of the fact that she hadn't eaten since he had known her. Suddenly, sick at his stomach, he reeled from the cell.

It wasn't until he had reached the spaceport and the *Alpha*

Actuary that his mind really started functioning again. When it did, he had an idea. He put in a call to the waiting Mickey Hatchet.

"I've got one last order for you, Mickey," he said. "You know my place on the asteroid?"

"Yeah," said the private eye.

"I want you to go there. Don't bother to knock or anything. Just slam into the first bedroom. There's a blonde in there who's been bothering me. You'll know how to handle her."

"Pow!" said Mickey Hatchet, pointing a finger.

"That's the idea. And thanks, Mickey."

"I'll take care of it," the lean private eye said grimly. "Dames." He cut the connection.

Manning took his ship up near the asteroid and waited until he saw the other ship land. He had a brief glimpse of the figure leaping from the ship and barreling into the house. Then, using the magnidrive on his own ship, he nudged the asteroid out of its orbit.

When he had his ship set for Terra, he finally put in a call to J. Barnaby Cruikshank.

"Manning, boy," J. Barnaby said when he recognized his caller. "I've been trying to locate you everywhere. That Fanya Sera—"

"I know," Manning said. "A fine guy you were. Willing to turn me into a table d'hôte in order to get your lousy case solved."

"You don't understand," J. Barnaby said. "I was going to warn you. I tried to, but you cut me off."

"Sure, but what about just turning her loose that way?"

"I've notified the police. What did you do about her?"

Manning chuckled. "I sent Mickey Hatchet over to see her and then I drove the asteroid out into space. You know the old gag about an irresistible force and an immovable object? Well, I've set it in motion. Mickey can't be seduced and Fanya can't be killed—but I'm betting on Mickey. That boy's got guts—even if they are where his brains ought to be."

J. Barnaby laughed with him. "That's my boy," he said. "Come on home. You'll feel better when you get here. I've just hired a new secretary."

Manning Draco's face lit up with interest.

"Unlike Mickey Hatchet, I like dames," he said. "But I got to admit I drew the line at this Fanya. I can't stand a dame who eats in bed."

GLOSSARY

Achernarians. "May your day be filled with blossoms" is a typical greeting on Achernar—not surprising when you consider that the life forms of Achernar evolved from insects of the Hymenoptera order. About 24 inches long, an Achernarian is equipped with four feet, the two front ones serving as an extra pair of hands when they walk upright. What had once been the front feet (the third pair of legs) had evolved into a pair of small hands with double thumbs, making the Achernarians skilled craftsmen. They have flightless wings, and wear a robe bearing the same gold and brown markings as the body, making it difficult to tell whether they are dressed or naked. Their rudimentary stingers are often concealed by fashionable rear aprons.

Acruxians. As nonmembers of the Galactic Federation, the Acruxians have a habit of making trouble among the Federation planets, trying to provoke war and looking for excuses to invade them. Hence the Acruxian saboteur in "Whistle Stop in Space" and "Mission to Mizar." A typical Acruxian, Dtilla Raishelle is rather intimidating: seven feet tall, with a huge cylindrical body supported on three sturdy legs. In full ceremonial dress, he bears a holster for his tri-blast weapon (see entry below). He has four tentacles, two at waist level and two at shoulder level. His two eye-stalks extend several inches above his head. For his tri-blast duel with Manning he sported the green skirt with ceremonial feathers worn by every Acruxian when dueling. In addition to their penchant for aggression, Acruxians are fond of concealing insults in such polite expressions as "I salute your going away."

Aircar. A vehicle that moves through the air instead of being confined to one plane of operation by gravity. It is propelled in various ways, including jet, isoprene, carbon, magnetic, and hand propulsion. The last method is not recommended by the Academy of Space Flight.

Aldebaranese. The people of Aldebaran evolved from the order of Chiroptera—bats. However, they have become completely humanoid in the process of evolution. The Aldebaranese females are especially attractive to Terran males, notably one glamorous anthropologist with a shapely figure and a chic hairdo of blond fur, who takes a shine to Manning. Although retaining none of the physical characteristics of their primitive ancestors, the Aldebaranese still share many of their ancient customs, including some rather unsettling feeding habits.

Algolians. As far as Terrans are concerned, every Algolian seems to look completely different from every other, so it is assumed that there are hundreds of different species on Algol. Nottyl Nadyl, for example, is no more than four feet tall, with a fat, round body, a small, partly bald head, and tentacles. But Encycla Grave, another Algolian, is eight feet tall, with a thin body and hair sticking out of his head like a rooster's tail. Each Algolian individual is a species unto himself... or could it be they are actually shape-shifting scammers?

Alpha Actuary. Manning Draco's personal space cruiser, incorporating many of his own designs. The ship's name is explained thus: *Alpha* because it is the first one of its kind, and *Actuary* because in the insurance business an actuary is one who computes risks and probabilities, and this ship does just that. Powered by a magnetic drive, it is equipped with all the latest gadgets, including an audio-reader for encyclotapes, a demagnetizer, a geoscope, an impulse-translator, a robosmith, and a telemeter. A miniature computer above the control panel flashes answers to questions fed into it, gives mathematical formulae, and displays varicolored graphs. No major weapons are aboard the ship, but a small energy gun enables Manning to hold off any direct attacks.

Audiophone. An old-fashioned telephone, sans visicast.

Canopusians. An inquisitive race of unknown origin, famed for their love of keyhole-peeping and gossip. The origin of Canopusians is unknown, as they seemed unrelated to any other life form. Their bodies and heads looked like inverted gourds, and they have two stubby legs and two tentacles midway on the body. Along with two humanoid eyes there is a third one on the end of a flexible eye-stalk, primarily used for peering around corners and into rooms. Canopus has no recognizable system of logic, as exemplified by their major city, Canopusia, where the streets run every which way and the street names often change in the middle of a block. No one can find their way around the city; thus the largest single profession on the planet is that of tour guide.

Caphians. A semi-humanoid race descended from the spotted bat. Wingless, with webbed fingers, tiny eyes, and large, paddle-like ears, they have adopted attributes of human culture such as Terran clothing, though sadly out of style. The Caph system, consisting of two planets in a single orbit around Caph, exists in what is known as a Time Fracture. Thus, while one year passes in the rest of the Galaxy, twenty years pass on Caph II, making the planet a popular resort destination, since you can spend ten months there, yet be gone only two weeks. On Caph I, one week equates to five years gone by in the outside universe. See "The Caphian Caper" in *Once Upon a Star,* vol. 1 of the Manning Draco stories.

Castorian Rummy. Castorian Rummy is played with three decks of 95 cards each—the regular seven suits of thirteen cards each and the four superjokers: Orbit, Comet, Asteroid, Nova. Each player receives 39 cards on the deal and simultaneously plays three games. Since it is possible to trade cards back and forth between one's three hands, considerable finesse is needed to play the game well. It is wisely said that one should never play Castorian Rummy with any form of life that has tentacles. See "The Merkian Miracle" in *Once Upon a Star.*

Chess, four-dimensional. Invented by Horace Homer Humptafield in 2983. Beginners are advised to start with Humptafield Parchesi in order to get used to thinking about infinity before moving on to chess. See "The Regal Rigelian" in *Once Upon a Star.*

Credit. Cash. A credit is worth approximately $1.75, Terran Old Currency.

Cybernetic mind-reading (M-R). A patented method of electronically recording the innermost thoughts of any intelligent being. The exact details have never been released because the process is so simple that anyone could build his own Cybernetic M-R out of odds and ends.

Demagnetizer. An inverse magnetic action that completely erases all magnetic flux in any object which is the focal point of the action. With all magnetism gone, the object falls apart. Used to destroy approaching meteors and (occasionally) a favorite uncle who has just made out his will.

Door-scanner. A method by which a door, using a variation of a platinum-iridium Sponge, can "remember" the structure of a regular visitor and "recognize" him on a return trip. While this is normally a fairly successful gadget, we have heard reports of such a door, on being faced by identical twins, short-circuiting and quickly making an ash of itself.

Encyclotape. A tape recording presenting detailed encyclopedic data on the culture of any planetary system, recited by a pleasant voice-over and played on an audio-reader aboard a spacecraft. The encyclotape aboard Manning Draco's *Alpha Actuary* provides crucial information on the fly about the diverse life forms and lifestyles of the multicultural Galaxy.

Fission. A method of reproduction used by life forms who haven't learned any better.

Fitzgerald-Lorentz. Also known as Lorentz-Fitzgerald Contraction. The theory that a moving body contracts in length along its line of motion, ultimately reaching zero length at the speed of light—making it impossible for any ship to exceed 186,326 miles per second. The Terran scientist Glomb was in the middle of finally proving this theory when a Terran pilot succeeded in traveling 377,424 miles per second. Glomb later became assistant janitor at the Terran Space Academy.

Galactic Federation. A political union of 107 planetary republics.

Galaxy. The Milky Way, containing several billion star systems.

Geoscope. A spaceship device that can display a three-dimensional photograph of any charted country or city in the Galaxy.

Humanoid. Nonhuman life that has evolved along similar lines to humans.

Impulse-translator. A device for converting any spoken language in the Galaxy into English, one of the three official languages of the Federation (along with Rigelian and Vegan).

Light-year. Astronomical measure of distance, the distance traveled by light in one year. Approximately 6,000,000,000,000 (six trillion) miles.

Mind shield. A mental force field that prevents a telepath from mind-reading. Many of the Galactic races possess this asset, notably the Martians, whose thoughts are especially hard to read, although they politely greet strangers with the phrase "My mind is open to you." The only Terran ever to develop a secondary mind shield to fend off aggressive mental probes was Manning Draco. *See also* Telepathy.

Mizar. The only inhabited planet in the system is Mizar I, a class B planet whose dominant humanoid race evolved from the amphibian duck-billed platypus. Though not mind-readers, the Mizarians are cryptesthesists, possessing the ability to know what an opponent's next move will be. Mizarians would thus be invincible in war—a matter of grave concern, considering their anti-Federation sentiments. Politically an empire, Mizar was ruled by his Royal Mostness, Emperor Alis Volat.

Monopolist. One who has obtained a charter from the government giving him a monopoly throughout a certain area of the Federation.

Muphridians. The nontelepathic beings of Muphrid are nearly like humans, although they evolved from the genus Paramecium. Kramu Korshay, an alluring Muphridian with cute blue head-feathers, tempted Manning in *Once Upon a Star* ("The Merakian Miracle"), but his romantic hopes were dashed when he found out about the reproductive process of ciliate protozoans.

Nyork. Phonetic rendering of "New York" (Terra), accepted as standard spelling in 2375.

Parsec. Approximately 3.3 light-years. A unit of measure seldom needed by the average person.

Polluxians. Bipedal reptoids with a formal, chivalrous culture who looked to Manning like alligators dressed up in human garb. The females conveniently reproduce by laying self-fertilizing eggs. Upon Manning was conferred the "honor" of being engaged to the Polluxian Emperor's daughter in *Once Upon a Star* ("The Polluxian Pretender"). Pollux is notorious for its popular local alcoholic drink, called dtseea, made of fermented swamp water.

Praesepe. A misty patch in the center of the constellation Cancer, where Manning Draco learned to be wary of accepting drinks on strange planets. His mistake on Praesepe I was in not realizing that their "limeade" was actually made from caustic quicklime and not from citrus fruits.

Rhine Cards. An ancient 20th-century device for testing telepathy, precognition, and other forms of ESP.

Regulusians. One of the non-telepathic races, the citizens of Regulus are closely related to the Star-Nosed Mole. The rather old-fashioned Regulusians do not use visicasts, quaintly preferring to be actually present at their entertainment instead of watching a reproduction of it.

Rigel Kentaurus. A star system approximately 542 light-years from Terra. The first planet in Rigel Kentaurus was the only completely self-sufficient system in the Galaxy and the seat of the Federation government; Rigelian is one of the three official Galactic languages. The entire planet was covered with buildings—government office buildings where the best best brains of 107 planets gather, as well as private homes and apartment houses, and a shopping center with several hotels. Solar University on Rigel Kentaurus was the alma mater of Manning Draco.

The fourth planet of the Rigel system is the only one inhabited. No extensive studies have been made, but it is known that Rigel IV has a completely criminal culture, based entirely on dishonesty. As the saying goes: If there's anyone more crooked than a Rigelian, it's another Rigelian. The infamous one-ton Rigelian known as Dzanku Dzanku was introduced in *Once Upon a Star* ("The Regal Rigelian"), where he joined with a Terran named Sam Warren to form the most double-crossing insurance sales team in the Galaxy.

It was well known that no Terran could penetrate a Rigelian's mind shield—until Manning Draco dared to lock minds with Dzanku Dzanku in *Once Upon a Star.*

Robosmith. A machine on Manning Draco's space cruiser for manufacturing trinkets. It came in handy when he had to land on a barbaric planet and placate the savages—or impress an attractive female passenger by crafting some jewelry on the spot.

Spaceport. A landing and launching field for spaceships.

Table d'hôte. A complete meal of several courses sold at a fixed price. This restaurant term is a French loan word that literally means "host's table."

Telepathy. Sometimes known as ESP. The universe is about equally divided between telepathic and non-telepathic races. The latter invariably have natural mind shields so that their minds could not be invaded by telepaths. The only exception to this was Terrans, whose minds could be invaded by anyone—but who wanted to know what they were thinking? Manning Draco was the only Terran with any degree of ESP. *See* Mind shield.

Terrans. Those inhabitants of Terra that are loosely classified as Man or Humankind. Once known as Earth, the planet Terra took its name in the 22nd century, probably from an ancient Roman deity of that name, who was considered the goddess of fertility. She was invoked in the most solemn oaths as Mother Earth (Tellus Mater) and as the common grave of all things. Long after this goddess vanished from religion, the inhabitants of this planet continued to observe a great variety of fertility rites (some of them quite bizarre), and it is believed that Terra may be the one goddess who continues to this day to exert a great influence.

Tri-blast. A three-barrelled blade-gun used in ceremonial duels between Acruxians, designed to amputate all three legs of the opponent.

Tzitsa. A lethal and telepathic form of crossword puzzle, like fencing with mental energy instead of foils. A game could last for months or even years if the opponents were evenly matched in mental strength and skill, which meant hundreds of thousands of horizontal and vertical strings of words. The game was invented by a Rigelian named Tzitsakele Tzitsakele. As explained by Manning in "The Caphian Caper" (in *Once Upon a Star*), the player who goes first has to give the definition of a word and the number of letters in it. But only one of these does he give vocally. The other is only a thought that his opponent has to pick out of his mind: "Then I can either work out what the word is or try to pull the word itself out of his mind from behind his secondary shield. While I'm doing that, my mental defenses must be let down to some degree, and he will then try to strike with enough mental force to kill me."

Unit. Small cash. The equivalent of 17.5 cents, Terran Old Currency. One hundred units equal one credit.

Vegans. The green-skinned race of the Vega system (not to be
confused with adherents of the prevailing ethical and dietary
practices of 21st-century humans). Known to space tourists
for their textiles and pastries. Vegan is one of the three official Galactic languages.

Visiphone. A telephone with video in the form of a visiscreen.

ABOUT THE AUTHOR

KENDELL FOSTER CROSSEN (1910–1981) was raised in Ohio and South Dakota, and worked in the Upson steel mills, in the Fisher Body Corporation, and as an insurance investigator. In 1937 he became associate editor at the old Munsey Company, where he edited a variety of magazines, including mystery, adventure, cheesecake, movie fan, and comics.

He began writing fiction in 1939. Under the pseudonyms Ken Crossen, Richard Foster, Bennett Barlay, and Kent Richards, he sold about two million words of mystery and adventure stories. In addition, he wrote radio scripts for *Suspense, Mystery Theatre, the Kate Smith Show,* and *The Saint.* His pulp character the Green Lama appeared under the name Richard Foster in *Double Detective* magazine as well as a series of comic books. His science fiction books include the futuristic novels *Once Upon a Star* (1953), *Year of Consent* (1954), and *The Rest Must Die* (1959), as well as two edited anthologies, *Adventures in Tomorrow* (1951) and *Future Tense* (1952). In the 1950s–1970s, under the names M.E. Chaber and Christopher Monig, Ken Crossen wrote a series of insurance detective and spy novels, notably those featuring the globe-trotting Milo March.

SCIENCE FICTION BY KENDELL FOSTER CROSSEN

PSEUDONYMS USED by Crossen for his science fiction include Richard Foster and Christopher Monig; variations of his own name are Kendell Foster Crossen (first name sometimes misspelled "Kendall"), Ken Crossen, Kendell F. Crossen, and Kendell Crossen.

The following stories appeared in the magazines *Amazing Stories, Double Detective, Dynamic Science Fiction, Fantasy and Science Fiction, Planet Stories, Science Fiction Adventures, Space Stories, Spaceway, Startling Stories,* and *Thrilling Wonder Stories.*

SHORT STORIES AND NOVELLAS

"Restricted Clientele." *Thrilling Wonder Stories,* February 1951, as by Kendell Foster Crossen; illus. by Peter Poultron. Featuring Michael Lance, Galactic Realty Corp. Also in *Adventures in Tomorrow* (1951).

"The Boy Who Cried Wolf 359." *Thrilling Wonder Stories,* April 1951, as by Kendell Foster Crossen (misspelled "Kendall"); illus. by Leo Ramon Summers. Featuring juvenile Bobby Edwards.

"The Last Touch of Venus." *Amazing Stories,* April 1951, as by Kendell Foster Crossen (misspelled "Kendall"); illus. by Edmond B. Swiatek. Featuring Dr. Gerald Gray, archeologist.

"The Merakian Miracle." *Thrilling Wonder Stories,* October 1951, as by Kendell Foster Crossen; illus. by Paul Orban. Featuring

Manning Draco, insurance investigator for Greater Solarian Insurance Co., Monopolated. Also in *Once Upon a Star* (1953, 2013).

"Love Story," as by Christopher Monig. *In Future Tense* (1952). Featuring Sir Cedric Langley, Emissary of the Royal Socialist Party.

"The Regal Rigelian." *Thrilling Wonder Stories*, February 1952, as by Kendell Foster Crossen; illus. by Paul Orban. Featuring Manning Draco, insurance investigator for Greater Solarian Insurance Co., Monopolated. Also in *Once Upon a Star* (1953, 2013).

"Things of Distinction." *Startling Stories*, March 1952, as by Kendell Foster Crossen; illus. by Virgil Finlay. Featuring Jerry Ransom, Account Executive with Denning, Dibble, Eeee & Nojul Advertising Agency. Also in *Future Tense* (1952).

"Ambassadors from Venus." *Planet Stories*, March 1952, as by Kendell Foster Crossen (misspelled "Kendall"); illus. by Vestal. Featuring Clyde Ellery, scientist.

"Passport to Pax." *Startling Stories*, July 1952, as by Kendell Foster Crossen; illus. by Virgil Finlay. Featuring Jair Holding, operator of the Personal Observation Bureau.

"The Hour of the Mortals." *Startling Stories*, August 1952, as by Kendell Foster Crossen; illus. by Alex Schomburg. Featuring Lucien B. Fenimore, Minister of Sanity.

"The Gnome's Gneiss." *Startling Stories*, September 1952, as by Kendell Foster Crossen; illus. by Alex Schomburg. Featuring Kevan MacGreene, who heard voices.

"The Polluxian Pretender." *Thrilling Wonder Stories*, October 1952, as by Kendell Foster Crossen; illus. by Alex Schomburg. Featuring Manning Draco, insurance investigator for Greater Solarian Insurance Co., Monopolated. Also in *Once Upon a Star* (1953, 2013).

"The Girl Next Door." *Thrilling Wonder Stories*, November 1952, as by Kendell Foster Crossen; illus. by C. H. Murphy. Featuring Lt. Mark Dana, 17th Precinct NYPD.

"The Caphian Caper." *Thrilling Wonder Stories,* December 1952, as by Kendell Foster Crossen; illus. by Alex Schomburg. Featuring Manning Draco, insurance investigator for Greater Solarian Insurance Co., Monopolated. Also in *Once Upon a Star* (1953, 2013).

"Get Along Little Unicorn." *Space Stories,* December 1952, as by Kendell Crossen. Featuring Oliver Greshold, Commissioner, Terra.

"Public Enemy." *Dynamic Science Fiction,* December 1952, as by Kendell Foster Crossen. Featuring Brad Raynor, Public Police Officer.

"Love That Air." *Startling Stories,* December 1952, as by Kendell Foster Crossen; illus. by Alex Schomburg. Featuring Jeff Reynolds, supervisor of nighttime visicasts for Solar Visicasting Company.

"My Old Venusian Home." *Startling Stories,* January 1953, as by Kendell Foster Crossen; illus. by Paul Orban. Featuring Pres. Jefferson Davis Masters and Sen. James Beauregarde of the New Confederate States of America. Reprinted in *S-F Yearbook* 1969.

"Assignment to Aldebaran." *Thrilling Wonder Stories,* February 1953, as by Kendell Foster Crossen. Featuring Prof. Laertes Kwang Solomon, Head of the Dept. of Impossible Events, Solar University on Kars. Reprinted in *Year's Best Science-Fiction Novels: 1954.*

"Halos, Inc." *Startling Stories,* April 1953, as by Kendell Foster Crossen; illus. by Alex Schomburg. Sequel to "Things of Distinction." Featuring Jerry Ransom, President of Halos, Inc., and Vice-President of Nojul, Ransom, Eeee and Dunning Advertising Agency.

"Whistle Stop in Space." *Thrilling Wonder Stories,* August 1953, as by Kendell Foster Crossen; illus. by Virgil Finlay. Featuring Manning Draco. Also in *Whistle Stop in Space: The Further Adventures of Manning Draco* (2013).

"The Closed Door." *Amazing Stories,* August-September 1953, as by Kendell Foster Crossen (misspelled "Kendall"). Featuring Detective Inspector Jair Calder, Solar Dept., Terran Division, Interplanetary Criminal Police Commission.

"Mission to Mizar." *Thrilling Wonder Stories,* November 1953, as by Kendell Foster Crossen; illus. by Alex Schomburg. Featuring Manning Draco. Also in *Whistle Stop in Space: The Further Adventures of Manning Draco, Volume 2* (2013).

"The Agile Algolian." *Thrilling Wonder Stories,* Winter 1953, as by Kendell Foster Crossen; illus. by Virgil Finlay. Featuring Manning Draco. Also in *Whistle Stop in Space: The Adventures of Manning Draco, Volume 2* (2013).

"His Head in the Clouds." *Startling Stories,* January 1954, as by Kendell Foster Crossen; illus. by Peter Poultron. Featuring Lancelot Pell, Operator, Clouds, Inc.

"Plague." *Science Fiction Adventures,* February-March 1954, as by Ken Crossen; illus. by Ebel. Featuring Eril of Acroma, Liege of the Star Fleet and Temporary Suzeran of the Hundred Worlds Council.

"The Green Earth Forever." *Spaceway,* June 1954, as by Christopher Monig; illus. by Charles Ross.

"The Golden Flask." *Fantasy and Science Fiction,* August 1962, as by Kendell F. Crossen. Featuring Eden Holloway, solitary drinker.

THE GREEN LAMA

The Green Lama: The Complete Pulp Adventures, 3 vols., as by Kendell Foster Crossen; reissues with bonus material (Boston: Altus Press, 2011–2012). Vol. 1: Primary illustrator V.E. Pyles, with Harry L. Parkhurst; Introduction by Will Murray. Vol. 2: Primary illustrator V.E. Pyles; Introduction by Michelle Nolan. Vol. 3: Primary illustrator V.E. Pyles, with Mike Fyles; Introduction by Martin Grams, Jr.; bonus story ("The Case of the Final Column") by Adam Lance Garcia.

"The Green Lama." *Double Detective,* April 1940, as by Richard Foster.

"Croesus of Crime." *Double Detective*, May 1940, as by Richard Foster; illus. by V.E. Pyles.

"Babies for Sale." *Double Detective*, June 1940, as by Richard Foster; illus. by V.E. Pyle.

"The Wave of Death." *Double Detective*, July 1940, as by Richard Foster; illus. by V.E. Pyles.

"The Man Who Wasn't There." *Double Detective*, August 1940, as by Richard Foster; illus. by V.E. Pyles.

"Death's-Head Face." *Double Detective*, September 1940, as by Richard Foster; illus. by V.E. Pyles.

"The Case of the Clown Who Laughed." *Double Detective*, October 1940, as by Richard Foster; illus. by V.E. Pyles.

"The Case of the Invisible Enemy." *Double Detective*, December 1940, as by Richard Foster; illus. by V.E. Pyles.

"The Case of the Mad Magi." *Double Detective*, February 1941, as by Richard Foster; illus. by V.E. Pyles.

"The Case of the Vanishing Ships." *Double Detective*, April 1941, as by Richard Foster; illus. by V.E. Pyles.

"The Case of the Fugitive Fingerprints." *Double Detective*, June 1941, as by Richard Foster; illus. by V.E. Pyles.

"The Case of the Crooked Cane." *Double Detective*, August 1941, as by Richard Foster; illus. by V.E. Pyles.

"The Case of the Hollywood Ghost." *Double Detective*, October 1941, as by Richard Foster; illus. by V.E. Pyles.

"The Case of the Beardless Corpse." *Double Detective*, March 1943, as by Richard Foster.

NOVELS AND STORY COLLECTIONS

Once Upon a Star: A Novel of the Future (New York: Henry Holt, 1953). Four humorous futuristic stories about Manning Draco, intergalactic insurance detective, in revised versions from *Thrilling Wonder Stories*. Reissued as *Once Upon a Star: The Adventures of Manning Draco*, vol. 1 (Boston: Altus Press, 2013).

Whistle Stop in Space: The Further Adventures of Manning Draco,
   vol. 2 (Boston: Altus Press, 2013). Reissue of three stories
   from *Thrilling Wonder Stories.*

Year of Consent, as by Kendell Foster Crossen (New York: Dell,
   1954). "Big Brother" dystopia set in 1990. Featuring Jerry
   Leeds, Bureau of Security and Control, Communication
   Administration Dept.

The Rest Must Die, as by Richard Foster (Greenwich, CT: Gold
   Medal, 1959). Featuring Bob Randall of the Chaber, Crossen
   and Monig Advertising Agency.

EDITED ANTHOLOGIES

Adventures in Tomorrow (New York: Greenberg, 1951)
Future Tense (New York: Greenberg, 1952)